And He Shall Be Called Nicholas

AND HE SHALL BE CALLED NICHOLAS

A Historical Novel

Marie Trotignon

*To my sister Betty –
who has always been my
greatest support
Love
Marie*

iUniverse, Inc.
New York Lincoln Shanghai

And He Shall Be Called Nicholas

Copyright © 2007 by Marie Trotignon

All rights reserved. No part of this book may be used or reproduced by any means, graphic, electronic, or mechanical, including photocopying, recording, taping or by any information storage retrieval system without the written permission of the publisher except in the case of brief quotations embodied in critical articles and reviews.

iUniverse books may be ordered through booksellers or by contacting:

iUniverse
2021 Pine Lake Road, Suite 100
Lincoln, NE 68512
www.iuniverse.com
1-800-Authors (1-800-288-4677)

Because of the dynamic nature of the Internet, any Web addresses or links contained in this book may have changed since publication and may no longer be valid.

Certain characters in this work are historical figures, and certain events portrayed did take place. However, this is a work of fiction. All of the other characters, names, and events as well as all places, incidents, organizations, and dialogue in this novel are either the products of the author's imagination or are used fictitiously.

ISBN: 978-0-595-45417-4 (pbk)
ISBN: 978-0-595-69686-4 (cloth)
ISBN: 978-0-595-89730-8 (ebk)

Printed in the United States of America

To my sons, Marc and Michael who each casts
a pretty impressive shadow of his own.

Acknowledgements

First, my thanks to Mark Pelton and Jim Lee without whose computer expertise, this book might never have gotten on its way.

Secondly, my appreciation to my writing and critiquing associates for their support and encouragement.

Last, but not least, my gratitude to my pioneer ancestors who, by example (and genetics) of courage and stubborn tenacity, have enabled me to meet life head on; to get up and keep going when things get tough.

Introduction

This book is based on actual events as recorded in the history of the Brisky family. Excerpts from documents, including Mr. Merck's will and the letters from Jasper during the Civil War, are from copies provided me by family members.

However, in order to write my story, it has been necessary to take certain liberties in characterization and the fictionalizing of some details. Therefore, as to which is fact and which is fiction, I will leave for you to decide.

NICHOLAS I
1746–1783

Chapter 1

▼

"Where were you last night?" The soft growl of Charles' voice invaded the pre-dawn darkness filling the small tent.

The lanky figure huddled in the bedroll next to his stirred, a sleepy grumble rising from amidst the tangled blankets.

"Nick!" Charles snapped impatiently.

With the swift reaction of the battle-wary, the soldier beside him sat abruptly upright, his hand already freeing his knife from its sheath. "What is it?" hissed Nick. "What's wrong?"

"That's what I want to know," Charles persisted. "Where were you last night?"

A ragged sigh released the tension knotting within Nick's chest. Lowering himself onto his elbow, he peered through the dim light toward his kinsman.

"I'm sorry if I caused you worry, little brother." Nick's austere features relaxed into a gentle smile of reassurance. "There was really no cause for your concern." Not waiting for a reply to his whispered apology, Nick continued. "I truly meant to return directly after we buried poor Raymond. But there is so much anguish and anger over this needless death of one of our countrymen. Several of us felt a need to meet … to somehow put an end to these terrible injustices we're being forced to endure."

"Oh, Nicholas. Do you think that was wise?" Despite the darkness, the tremor in Charles' voice betrayed his alarm. "If you'd been seen or overheard ... you know there are spies all over camp. You could have been shot, just like poor Raymond."

Hearing his brother's distress, Nick felt a pang of remorse. "We were most discreet, dear Charles," he soothed. "Surely you know I would do nothing to endanger us further."

Yet, in spite of his offered words of reassurance, Nick feared Charles was right. The midnight meeting had been a rash and dangerous act; one that could easily have worsened an already intolerable situation.

A distraught Charles raked fingers through his dark unkempt hair, grown long and tangled from neglect. "We should never have left France," he grumbled. "We'd not be in this terrible situation."

"Now, Charles," Nick objected. "You know that's not right. You know as well as I we were being driven to poverty with the high taxes King Louis was levying. His total disregard for the welfare of the commoner can only lead to a revolution. This was our chance to escape all that."

"What you say may be true," Charles interrupted. "But don't forget, our family bears a royal title awarded for outstanding service in the French army. Surely that guarantees us some privileges above the commoner."

"La Briskey!" Nick spat the family's titled name into the tent's musty interior. "Do you really think that would make a difference? Our families would starve right along with everyone else."

"What about our families?" Charles challenged, a frown marring his usually delicate features. "When we joined these troops being deployed to New France, we promised our families we'd send for them; promised them a better life in the New World. Now they starve in France while we sit over here in a British prison camp, faring no better than they."

"I know, I know," Nick sighed. "But we had no idea our troops were so poorly trained or our leaders would make so many wrong decisions. But we're not alone, little brother. Last night I learned nearly four thousand of our men were taken captive during Montgomery's disastrous battle at Quebec."

"And look at us," Charles persisted, his voice rising in anger. "Four thousand French prisoners, half of us suffering from scurvy or dysentery, thrown into camp alongside the British, our enemy. Do you realize there are two *Englishmen* in the tent next to ours?"

"We're not the only ones disillusioned, Charles," Nick countered. "At last night's meeting, I learned many of the British soldiers are also becoming disturbed over camp conditions. Believe me, Charles, it is not just our countrymen. Any soldier, British as well as French, is being turned in by camp spies, shot for merely voicing discontent."

"You knew this, even after Raymond was shot for merely complaining about the poor medical treatment, and you still held that meeting?"

"In honesty, Charles, it was a most informative gathering." Nick pressed on, hoping to further soothe his brother's fears. "We discovered this same dissatisfaction with British rule also exists in the New Colonies to the south. There are those among us who would take advantage of this unrest; perhaps join forces with the Colony dissenters.

"No!" Charles shook his head in stubborn defiance. "No, I refuse to discuss it."

"Please," Nick laid a beseeching hand upon the shoulder of the slender man beside him. "Hear me out, mon frere. We cannot continue …"

The words perished unspoken upon his tongue as a rasping sound reached them from outside the tent, the sound of something or someone brushing against the canvas. His own thumping heart frantically crowding into his throat, Nick held up a hand to silence his brother who stared at him open-mouthed, eyes grown wide in his now ashen face.

In the next instant, the flap of their tent was flung open and two figures crowded into their cramped quarters. Nick's fingers closed quickly about the smooth bone handle of his knife.

"Wait! We come as friends!" Though the words were spoken in French, Nick recognized the unmistakable clipped accent of an Englishman. "Tell me, quickly, what were you speaking of just now?" the voice urged.

The wan light of the approaching day filtered through the tent's worn fabric revealing the fear in his brother's glance. Nick felt the cold fungus of fear sprouting in his own chest.

"Who are you? What do you want?" Nick's demand rumbled low in his throat.

"My name is Jasper." It was the stocky, bearded intruder who responded. Then, with an impatient gesture toward his younger, clean-shaven companion, "and this is Newton. Please," he implored turning back to Nick, "I must tell you, I fear you may be in great danger." He hurried on, reverting to his own English language. "As Newton and I were leaving our tent just now, we spotted two blokes lurking outside your tent, apparently listening to whatever you were discussing. They dashed off toward headquarters at the sight of us."

Nick was already jamming his feet into his boots, pleased to note that his brother was quickly following his lead.

"I can only assume your conversation was one that would prove not to your best interest," Jasper observed as Nick and Charles hastily began gathering their belongings. "So be it, then," he announced as if having arrived at some decision of his own. "No," He quickly laid a restraining hand upon that of Charles who was reaching for the white jacket of his uniform. "Leave that. We don't want anything that will identify you as a French soldier."

"We?" One arm already thrust into the sleeve of his own jacket, Nick whirled upon the Englishman.

"I believe it's quite obvious. All four of us must now leave this camp. Perhaps with Newton and I as your apparent guards, there is less possibility of detection." There was a quiet urgency in Jasper's voice. "I suggest we leave as quickly as possible."

Nick's eyes narrowed. These men were English, the enemy. Could they be trusted? Should they be trusted? The Frenchman met the unwavering gaze of the Englishman who, without doubt, had just saved their lives. With a barely perceptible nod, "So be it," Nick whispered softly.

So it was, the unlikely alliance was formed and four shadowy figures crept furtively from the Frenchmen's tent, slipped quietly through the pale, predawn light shrouding the camp and disappeared into the welcome oblivion of the forest.

Chapter 2

By mid-morning, the four fugitives had put a comfortable distance between themselves and the British army camp. Only then did they pause to rest and assess their situation. There seemed to be no question among them but that the path they chose would be one taking them south, one that should eventually bring them to the Colonies.

"It behooves us to keep to the wooded areas a little longer," suggested Jasper. "While it will interfere with the speed of our journey, I do suspect we still need concern ourselves with the possibility of detection."

"You are right, of course," Nicholas agreed. "We would receive no mercy should we be apprehended now."

The journey proved to be more difficult than they'd anticipated. Lack of familiarity with the terrain presented their first problem. They'd already traveled several miles along their chosen path when they discovered it had brought them to the edge of a large swampy quagmire.

"Perhaps if we separate," Jasper suggested, "we can find a way around this swamp. Newton, you and Charles investigate the west perimeter, Nicholas and I will search to the east. Let us return to this point within an hour's time.

Unfortunately, their efforts provided no more than added frustration. At the hour's end, they had found no solid ground for crossing and were left with no alternative but to reluctantly retrace their steps in search of a more passable route south.

The second and most disturbing problem was the task of foraging for food. Their one meal a day, consisting of the meager collection of wild berries they were able to gather proved to be less than satisfying, convincing them of the need for a more substantial form of nourishment. While the Englishmen carried their muskets with them when they slipped out of camp, use of those firearms was both impractical and dangerous. They realized they wold have to rely upon trapping skills and fleetness of foot if they were to upgrade their food supply.

Adding to their problems was the threat of detection and capture, not only by the British, but also by Indians. Having witnessed, first hand, the unfair treatment Indians often suffered at the hands of the British, the fugitives had no doubt the Indian's hatred for the white man would be extended to include them.

Their fears were nearly realized on the second day into their journey. Dusky shadows of early evening were already rising from the forest floor when Newton spotted the little gray rabbit. Determined it would be their day's meal, he scrambled up a small knoll in pursuit of the fleeing cottontail. Leaping to the crest of the embankment, he seemed on the verge of accomplishing his mission when he hesitated, mid-stride. In the next instant, he flung himself to the ground, frantically waving away his companions who, thinking he had pounced upon his prey, were preparing to join him. Slithering and crab-walking his way to the bottom of the slope, Newton struggled to his feet. Lifting his finger to his lips, he silently mouthed the warning, "Indians."

Cautiously, lest the snap of a branch or rustle of a bush betray them, the four men crept back into the protective company of night shadows now furtively congregating beneath the tall firs. Not until they were safely out of earshot did Newton attempt to share what he'd witnessed from the top of the knoll.

"Could be a hunting party," he whispered. "There were four, maybe five of them, squatting around a campfire."

Charles' voice trembled as he searched his brother's face for reassurance. "What if there are more of them, Nick, maybe still out hunting in these woods?"

Nicholas could only shake his head. "We've no way of knowing. Perhaps it would be safest to remain where we are for the night."

Their backs braced against one another, the weary men crouched in a circle upon the mossy earth, its chilling dampness creeping through the inadequacy of their clothing. Nicholas slipped an arm across Charles' shivering shoulders, drawing his brother close in order to share the warmth of his own body. Unable to build a fire lest its smoke betray them, the four fugitives could only huddle together through the long, fearful night. Their misery was further aggravated by the tantalizing odor of roasting rabbit drifting across the cold night air, assailing their nostrils, setting their empty stomachs to growling.

The inquisitive fingers of a mid-morning sun were probing among the overhead branches before the four bone-chilled soldiers grew brave enough to leave their place of hiding and resume their journey. It was well into late afternoon on the third day of travel when they first noticed a gradual thinning of the stand of trees lining their path. It wasn't long before they realized the absence of timber was not a whim of nature but the obvious work of man. Bearing the definite scars inflicted by an axe, an army of weathered tree stumps marched ahead of them to the edge of a clearing.

Caution once again became their mentor as the foursome paused to study the unexpected scenario opening before them. Dominating the center of clearing was a roughly hewn log cabin, blue-gray smoke drifting from its stone chimney. Alongside the structure, in a field perhaps fifty meters in length, tall stalks of corn nodded their bearded heads in the warm sun. Beyond, in an area double the size of the cornfield, a sea of wheat undulated in the gentle afternoon breeze. To the west of the cabin, split rail fencing enclosed a corral. Off to one side stood a stone well, the promise of cool waters dripping from a wooden bucket hanging from its shaft.

"Settlers?" His uncertainty was obvious in Jasper's voice.

Nicholas raised his eyebrows in response. "How then would you choose," he asked of the Englishman. "Would you have us seek another path and be on our way?" His glance slid across the faces of his two other companions; noted weariness replacing the hope that flitted there a moment before. "Perhaps we could rest here a bit," he suggested. "These settlers may know of a shorter route to the Colonies."

Stepping from the shelter of trees, they'd advanced but a few steps when the door of the cabin swung open and a woman stepped forth. Dark hair stretched into a bun at the nape of her neck accentuated the grim, sternness of her face. A small child clung to her gingham skirts. Shoulders squared, she faced them defiantly. In her hands, she gripped a long rifle, its muzzle aimed directly at them.

Aware of the frightening apparition the four of them must present; unshaven, mud from three days travel staining their clothing, Nicholas slowly lifted both hands, palms outward.

"Please," he urged softly. "Do not be frightened. We come in peace."

Her gaze not leaving his face, the woman stepped sideways to the corner of the cabin.

The barrel of the rifle did not waver as, freeing one hand, she reached for the rope dangling from a brass bell suspended above her. Three strong yanks on its cord and the afternoon was splintered by the bell's frantic, reverberating cries for help.

Chapter 3

▼

Four bowls, once filled with a hearty rabbit stew, now sat empty, nearly all trace of its savory gravy wiped clean by huge slabs of homemade bread. At the end of the wooden table, Victor watched his guests, smiling his pleasure at their obvious enjoyment of the meal just finished. His wife's urgent summons for help had quickly brought the wiry Frenchman and his two teenage sons from the fields they were preparing for a new crop of rye. Once he'd learned two of the intruders upon his land were French soldiers and heard the story of how the two Englishmen had saved their lives, Victor sent his reluctant sons back to their chore. Inviting the four fugitives into his home, he insisted upon sharing what was to have been his family's evening meal.

Victor's smile widened as sighs of satisfaction drifted about the table. "My Suzanne, she is a good cook, no?"

Nicholas returned Victor's smile with one of contentment. "You've been most generous, sir. We never expected to come upon such good fortune in a place such as ..." Nicholas hesitated, fearful his implication might have offended their benefactor.

"Ah, you are surprised to find civilized people in this wilderness, eh?" Victor nodded his head in understanding. "You will be more surprised to learn we are not alone," he added. "We have many neighbors here, ex-soldiers like you. Frenchmen and, yes, Englishmen too, all starting a new life in the New World."

The four men, having settled back in their chairs, now leaned forward. "How so, my friend?" Jasper urged.

Placing his arm gently around the small child who'd moved from her mother's skirts to her father's side, Victor launched into a dissertation of what he identified as the 'habitant program.' A great number of French soldiers, he explained, weary and disillusioned by poorly organized battles, were leaving at the end of their enlistment to return to their homeland. In hope of detaining as many of them as possible, the French government was offering land grants to French soldiers with one stipulation. They must agree to plant crops of grain upon the land thus serving a two-fold purpose. It would, Victor explained, insure by population, France's foothold in New France and, at the same time, help offset the country's dangerously diminishing supply of wheat, rye and corn.

"A clever plan," Nicholas observed. "And a wonderful opportunity for those able to take advantage of it."

"Ah, yes, a clever plan." Victor's teeth flashed white beneath his dark mustache. "So clever, the English are now offering it to their men." He turned his gaze to include the four men seated at his table. "Perhaps it is something you would give thought to," he suggested. "There is still much land to be had in this community."

"Exactly where are we, the location of this community, I mean?" Jasper's interest was obviously aroused.

"Ah, that depends," Victor parried. "If you are French, we are south of Montreal. If you are English, then we are north of the Colonies."

Jasper turned to Nicholas his question unspoken but apparent.

Nicholas shook his head. "A wonderful opportunity, yes. But we, Charles and I ..." he glanced apologetically toward his brother. "We left families in France."

"Aha, my friend, there is more." The Frenchman's eyes twinkled with his enthusiasm. "The government is also offering free passage, not only to young women who would become wives of bachelor soldiers, but also to those families left back in France. More French families, more French babies." Glancing furtively toward his wife, Victor lowered his voice. "It is what some are calling "Victory of the Cradle."

"Oh, Nick!" Charles face was alight with excitement, his eyes bright with tears at the thought of seeing his family again.

* * * *

In the weeks that followed, Nick would come to believe that the confusion created by Montgomery's devastating defeat at Montreal, the same confusion that left Nick and Charles bivouacked alongside their equally disgruntled enemy, was now working to their advantage. As an extra precaution, Nick and Charles dropped the royal title from their name; made a slight change in its spelling. Still, their mere status as ex-soldiers seemed enough to secure them land grants in this small community. Jasper and Newton, perhaps aided by the same confusion, were also able to claim land nearby.

Once the land grants had been issued, the two brothers turned their attention toward extraditing their families from France. With Victor's help, they were able to arrange passage for Nicholas' wife, Elisa and Charles' wife, Yvonne and two young daughters, Nicole and Collette. While the procedure proved to be an easy one, the process was slow. It would be several months before their loved ones could join them in the New World. Meanwhile there was land to be cleared, cabins to build. Between them, Nicholas and Charles were able to acquire one plow horse to help them till the soil for the grain crops needing to be planted.

Finally word arrived, the ship carrying immigrants from France was expected to reach Montreal within the week. From there its passengers would be escorted to Montpelier, a small community near the granite deposits on the Winooski River where they would be met by their families and sponsors. Leaving their homesteads under the watchful care of their friend Victor, Nicholas and Charles hitched their horse to a borrowed wagon and set out for Montpelier.

Unfortunately, their arrival failed to coincide with that of their families and so the two brothers were forced to spend the next few anxious few days nurturing their impatience. At long last, the convoy bearing their loved ones arrived. Nicholas once again held Elisa in his arms; Charles was able to gather his family to him, a tearful wife and two young daughters who shyly surrendered to their father's embrace.

It would have been a good life for the two Frenchmen but for one small, bitter pill. Concentrating upon other acquisitions, the French government abandoned their claim upon the New World and withdrew their army. The land where Nick and Charles settled, along with the Colonies to the south, fell once again under British rule.

Chapter 4

"Oncle Nick! Oncle Nick!"

Their excited shouts fleeing before them, two little girls, dark curls bouncing, raced across the uneven stubble of the yard. Dropping to one knee, Nick opened his arms as his young nieces flung themselves at him.

"Ah, bonjour mes petite cherie," he cried, gathering the giggling youngsters in his embrace. "Vos papa? Where is your papa?"

Glancing across the tousled heads, he caught sight of Charles emerging from the doorway of the cabin. "Ah, mon frere." Nick rose quickly to his feet to accept the embrace of his brother. "Bonjour, bonjour."

Bonjour, mon frere. What brings you to us this midday hour?"

"Why else but to check on the young rascal who is my brother," Nick grinned as he delivered a playful punch to Charles' shoulder. In the next instant Nick's smile was replaced by a look of concern. He glanced toward the two children dancing in happy circles around them. "May we speak in private? There is something I wish to share with you."

"Nicole, Collette." Charles spoke softly to his daughters. "Go to your maman. I will return shortly." The youngsters dutifully obeyed, skipping back to the cabin while Nick and Charles turned toward the privacy of the wheat fields. "What is it Nick?" Charles urged. "Is it Elisa? I know she has not been happy these past months. Is that why you come to us at this hour of the day, to speak of Elisa?"

"No, no, it is not that," Nick reassured his brother. "Though, truly, her unhappiness does distress me. It has been difficult for her. Her ways are still those of France. She cannot understand how we are able to transfer our allegiance, even to rejecting our royal title. She does not comprehend the greatness of the opportunities awaiting us in this new country." Nick shook his head. "Ah, but that is not why I come to you today. It is of a different nature, that which I wish to share." He pulled a sheet of paper from his pocket. "A messenger from Boston has delivered it to me this morning." He handed over the pamphlet for his brother's inspection.

Charles scanned the leaflet then turned questioning eyes toward Nick. "'Common Sense' by a Thomas Paine?"

"As we both know, there is much unrest within the colonies concerning our taxes, our free trade laws being controlled by a government across the sea from us," Nick explained. Nick nodded toward the pamphlet in Charles' hand. "It is quite a powerful bit, this publication of Mr. Paine's. I strongly feel it will lead us into a revolution."

"And ...?" Charles raised a questioning eyebrow.

"I wish only to alert you, my brother. If fighting does erupt, well, a decision will need to be made."

Sensing the implication of Nick's words, Charles frowned. "But it would mean leaving our families again, our farms," he argued.

"I would remind you, mon frere, we are soldiers first, farmers second; trained to fight for the protection and betterment of our country. This, now, is our country."

*　*　*　*

Once again the four ex-soldiers sat across a crude wooden table from one another. On this occasion, however, it was Nick's table, Nick's cabin. On the rough planks between them lay copies of Tom Paine's publications 'Crisis' and 'Tis Time to Part.'

"Newton and I intend to set off on the morrow," Jasper had just announced.

"We plan to journey southward where we hope to join up with General Washington's chaps."

Nick studied the serious faces turned expectantly toward him. For a moment, his gaze darted toward the stone fireplace where his wife, Elisa, eyes averted, doggedly stirred the bubbling contents of a pot hanging above a crackling fire. The warm surge of love crowding around his heart quickly gave way to a chill of sadness. He knew, without doubt, the decision he was about to make would distress her. Still, he knew there could be no other choice for him.

Suppressing a sigh, Nick glanced toward his brother, noted his nod of assent then turned to meet the question in Jasper's eyes. "Can a virtuous man do otherwise?" he responded. "Of course, Mon Ami, Charles and I will journey with you."

While he sensed an immediate relief in those seated at the table, he was aware of the sudden stiffening in the back Elisa turned toward him. Once plans were made for the next day's departure, chairs scraped back and the three men filed quietly from the cabin. Nick was left alone with Elisa. Rising from the table, he moved to his wife's side, gently touched her shoulder. He felt her muscles tighten beneath his hand.

"It is not as before, Mi Amour, when it was necessary for you to remain in France" he argued softly. "This time, I will only be a short distance away. I will return often to check on your well-being." His assurance met with silence. "I will be here in the spring to plant the grain," he promised. "And, if the fighting is not over, I will return again at harvest time."

"Oh? You would become, then, a 'sunshine patriot? A 'summer warrior'?"

Nick flinched at the unfamiliar sharpness of sarcasm in her voice. He knew his wife spoke of the label Tom Paine attached to farmer/soldiers who often left the battlefield; returning only after their fields were plowed and planted.

"If need be, yes, Bein Aimee," Nick's responded quietly. "I will become either, if necessary, so that I may serve both my country and my family."

* * * *

During their first two years with the Militia, Nick and Charles kept this promise. They returned home each spring to plant their crops and again at harvest time. But as the war escalated, the fighting grew more intense, the opportunity to revisit their farms was no longer an option. There followed a period of five years when the brothers did not see their families, or their homes. Surrounded by the horror of the battlefield, they saw only the misery of their compatriots. While there were veterans from the French and Indian wars among their ranks, most of the men were untrained, undisciplined, abandoning their regiments once their enlistment elapsed, regardless of impending skirmishes. Yet, like many others, Nicholas and Charles remained, enduring the bitterness of battle.

They found little encouragement in General Washington's judgement when, upon reviewing his troops, he deemed them unfit to fight, three thousand nearly naked men, many of them suffering from typhus and smallpox.

"It is true, we have suffered many defeats." Nick attempted to assuage his brother's despair. "But we have also known many victories."

Yet, for Nicholas and Charles, none of those victories brought the glories promised in Tom Paine's literature. Instead, the two brothers witnessed the pain of a fellow compatriot, his leg ripped off by a musket ball, shared the miseries of their fellow battle weary soldiers, feet wrapped in rags for lack of shoes, clothing little more than remnants of material hanging from their emaciated bodies. The battlefield brought only cold, mud and hunger; for Nick, the most unbearable being the terrible, terrible hunger.

Often, they had nothing more to eat than "fire bread," a tasteless flour paste baked atop a hot rock, or immature green corn they'd pilfered from some farmer's field. Ever to plague Nick's memory was the Thanksgiving their dinner consisted of no more than one-half gill of rice and a tablespoon of vinegar. Unforgettable too, was the emptiness of forfeited victories; battles when their half-starved troops, having successfully routed the enemy, chose to plunder the enemy's larder rather than pursue the retreating Tories.

Somehow, through it all, Nicholas and Charles managed to remain together. They had long since lost track of their friends, Jasper and Newton, though a rumor did circulate through camp of an outstanding act of bravery by a Sergeant Jasper in the battle of Charleston.

Sometime after the battle of Yorktown, their health destroyed, bodies broken, the two brothers wandered homeward. Nick's injured leg, still harboring a bullet from a British Tory's pistol, made their progress slow and painful. Only the anticipation of their homecoming kept their feet upon the path. Once they left the Colonies and drew near the settlements of the habitants, uneasiness began to nibble at the edge of their eagerness. Clearing after clearing stood empty, fields gone to seed for lack of care, once inhabited cabins reduced to ashes. Icy fear became their traveling companion.

*   *   *   *

"Mon Dieu! Mon Dieu!"

Ignoring the burning fire in his leg, Nick struggled toward the edge of the clearing where Charles stared in horror at the charred remains of his home. Clutching a spindly sapling for support, Nick eased himself down to where his brother, arms wrapped about himself, now huddled in shock. Like an acid residue of gunpowder upon his tongue, Nick would long taste the bitterness of their homecoming. It brought them no joy for there were no loved ones to greet them.

It was Victor who provided the terrible details. One of the fortunate few, his home still stood but his crops were only a memory. While his wife sat in a chair across the room, her head bent over a piece of mending, their friend and neighbor began his explanation. "My sons, morte. Both dead." It was a moment before he seemed able to trust himself to speak again. He waited as his young daughter, eyes downcast, moved about the table to refill their cups with hot tea. "We lived in constant fear of marauding Indians," he finally confessed. He turned toward the younger of his two companions. "Ah, Charles, mon ami. My heart wishes to burst with sorrow for what I will tell you. You must be told, it was an Iriquois war party responsible for the burning of your cabin." He hesitated. "But only after massacring your family."

"Mon Dieu, Mon Dieu," Charles wept into hands covering his face.

Nick's eyes, dulled by grief, searched the face of his friend. He forced the words from numb lips. "My wife, Elisa, can you tell me what has become of her?"

"Ah, so tragique." Tears glistened upon Victor's cheeks. "Elisa? She is dead, but it was the typhus sickness that took her." Victor paused, then added softly, "Mon Ami, there is more you must be told." His voice faltered as he met his friend's fearful gaze. "Five years have passed since last you were allowed to return for harvest," he went on. "It was then, after you rejoined your patriots, your wife bore you a son, a son she called Nicholas." He laid a gentle hand on Nick's arm. "Neighbors have taken him, Mon Ami. I know not where."

In the terrible days that followed, Nicholas and Charles remained with the family of their friend. Although struggling with his own bereavement, Nick became deeply concerned about his brother. Weakened by the ravages of war, Charles, now totally devastated by grief, seemed unable to cope with his overwhelming loss. Nicholas feared it might destroy him.

* * * *

Dew still lay heavy upon the grass as Nicholas stepped out into the pale light of the new day. Seated upon a stump at the edge of the corral, Charles stared, unseeing, into the pink clouds of sunrise. Crossing the yard, Nicholas laid a hand gently upon his brother's shoulder.

"Bonjour, mon frere." His brother remained silent. "My dear Charles, it is time for us to make plans, decide what we must do, where we will go. We need to...." He hesitated, unspoken words trembling upon his lips.

Charles had turned to face his brother, staring up at him from hollow, empty eyes. "Please, Nicholas," he pleaded. "Let us go home, back to France. I wish to see vous Mere again. And vous Pere."

Dropping to his good knee, Nicholas gathered his brother's frail body in his arms. "Do not distress yourself, dear brother," he whispered. "Somehow, I will get us back to France. I promise, you will see our mama and papa again."

Chapter 5

▼

Victor listened in silence as Nick announced his decision to return to France. Although his lips pressed into a thin, hard line of disapproval, their friend offered no word of discouragement to the two brothers.

"You will take one of my horses, Mon Ami," he insisted. "It will make the journey an easier one."

Nick was painfully aware of the sacrifice in Victor's offer. With only one horse to assist him, restoration of his fields would take much longer. But Nick also knew Charles, in his condition, could never make the journey on foot. A lump crowding into his throat, Nick clasped the hand of his dear friend. "Merci, Mon Ami," he whispered. "Merci."

Their journey back through the colonies had been a slow one, Charles growing weaker with each tedious mile. By the time they reached the seaport town of Charleston, Nicholas could no longer deny the seriousness of his brother's illness. A heaviness in his heart, he recognized the dreaded symptoms having witnessed them too often upon the battlefield. It was the fever. Charles had typhoid.

* * * *

Nick twisted the tattered wet towel, its excess moisture dribbling back into the chipped enamel basin. Carefully, he pressed the cool damp cloth against the hot, feverish brow of the frail figure huddled among the tangled blankets on the narrow bed. Dipping the corner of a second cloth into the bedside basin of water, Nick gently daubed the pale, parched lips as they moved in silent anguish, giving soundless voice to unknown nightmares.

"Rest, dear brother," Nick whispered as he carefully rearranged the thin, discarded blankets which, until a few moments ago, Charles had clutched to himself for warmth.

"I will remain with you until this terrible sickness has passed."

Wearily, Nick eased himself into his vigil chair beside the bed, careful to favor the leg still harboring the British Tory's bullet. He gazed down into his brother's once handsome face, now ravaged by hardship, fever and grief. Nick quickly blinked away the moisture that stung his eyes.

"These are the times that try men's souls".

Tom Paine's words crowded into Nick's thoughts. Once again he was seated at the crude wooden table where the decision to take part in the revolution had first been made. What, he wondered, had become of their friends, Jasper and Newton with whom they'd set out to join forces with General Washington? Were they still alive? Or were they gone, like so many comrades; like Charles' family; like his own wife, his child?

A soft moan intruded upon Nick's reflections, bringing him quickly to his feet. Ignoring the sharp spasm of pain shooting through his leg, he moved to the bedside intending to tuck the blankets more firmly about the occupant's shivering form. Instead, he lowered himself onto the narrow cot. "I am here, dear brother," he soothed. "I am here." He wrapped his arms about Charles until his own warmth had driven the shuddering chills from his brother's body.

Nick's thoughts drifted back to those earlier days of incendiary patriotism. *"The harder the conflict, the more glorious the triumph."* Those, too, had been Tom Paine's words. But where was that glory now, Nick wondered as he hugged the, frail wasted body at his side. An unexpected wave of bitterness swept through him. Where was that glory now, for Charles, for himself, for any of them?

A sharp twinge of pain snatched Nick from the torment of his memories as his injured leg protested its discomfort. Careful not to disturb his brother, Nick eased himself up from the inadequate bed. Restlessly, he paced the small room until the stiffness in his leg forced him to his vigil chair where unwelcome memories rejoined him.

Perhaps General Washington's accusation was right, he conceded. They were unfit to fight. But they had fought and they had been victorious. They'd won the independence, though it proved to be dearly bought. He and Charles paid with the lives of their families, with their own health, yet now, they were forfeiting that independence, leaving it behind. Nick sighed, closing his eyes against an overwhelming weariness. How could he deny his grieving brother's plea to return to France?

Nick knew a pang of regret as his thoughts turned to the selfless generosity of his friend Victor; to the horse he'd planned to barter for their passage to France. Instead, he'd traded the emaciated animal for lodgings in this tiny hotel room where he hoped to nurse his brother back to health.

Nick dragged his hand across tired burning eyes. He'd lost count of the number of days they'd been closeted in these cramped quarters. He glanced toward Charles. His brother seemed to be resting easier. Perhaps the fever had broken. Leaning forward, he laid his hand upon Charles' forehead, then gasped at the cold clamminess greeting his palm. Swiftly, he knelt beside the bed, his ear close to his brother's pale, blue-tinged lips. Holding his own breath, Nick listened for the sound of Charles' breathing. There was none.

The cruel fist of grief tightened its ruthless fingers about Nick's heart. Pain filled his chest, forcing tears into his eyes, tears that spilled, unheeded, down his cheeks. It was finished. Charles was gone.

Chapter 6

▼

"Nicholas! Nicholas, get back here! Get away from that man!"

The woman's shrill voice pierced the mid-morning air, driving sharply into the vacuum of Nick's mind as it lay vegetating in the quagmire of his grief. Slouched against the building where he'd slept the night before, hunched protectively about his misery, Nick lifted his head at the familiar sound of his name upon a woman's lips. His once-dull eyes brightened hopefully. But instead of the stern face of a scolding wife, he found himself looking into the inquisitive eyes of a cherub-faced little boy.

"Nicholas Brisky! Do you hear me? Get away from that filthy man!"

His curiosity apparently satisfied, the dark-haired little adventurer scampered back to the woman standing at the edge of the sidewalk.

Something stirred inside Nick's lethargic brain, prodding it from inertia. *What had she called him, the little boy? Nicholas, Nicholas Brisky? But HE was Nicholas Brisky.* Confused, he struggled to his feet; lurched forward, his hand outstretched toward these intruders upon his sleep. The woman snatched the arm of the child, drawing him close to her. Nick opened his mouth to speak but his throat was dry; his lips moved soundlessly.

"Wait, wait," he managed to croak. But the woman was already dragging her young charge to the safety of distance.

Nick stumbled after them, then collapsed weakly against the building. His dazed mind groped through the past few moments of confusion. *The woman had called the boy Nicholas? And what was it she called him ... a filthy man?* Glancing down, Nick gasped, suddenly appalled at the sight of the unkempt clothing covering his thin, emaciated body. Gingerly, he raked a hand across his whiskered jaw, fingering the matted nest of his beard. He searched again through the fog shrouding his memory. *Mon Dieu! When had this happened?* The pain he had exiled now jolted through him. *Charles, his dear brother, gone! Gone, too, his wife, taken by the fever; his only son*, lost *to him forever. His son?* The morning's confrontation flashed before him. Was it possible his son was alive, here in Charleston? The fog was gone, his mind clear. The little boy, the one she'd called Nicholas, he was maybe five years old, about the same age as....

He had to find them, find that woman and the little boy. A rush of shame washed over Nick as he glanced again at his pathetic appearance. But not like this, he vowed. Not like this. First, he would have to make himself presentable.

He had no money to replace his neglected clothing, but no matter. A few blocks east the Cooper River made its way to the harbor. Its waters would at least remedy the issue of cleanliness. His fingers struggled through the tangled growth covering his scalp. What could he do about his hair, his beard? Temporarily filled with concerns of his appearance, his thoughts now churned ahead to the moment he could begin the search for his son.

* * * *

His clothing, obviously intended for a man of larger proportions, hung loosely from his too-thin frame. His scuffed boots bore the scars of many months wear. The clothes were a generous gift from the woman at the restaurant where he'd solicited a handout. The boots were the same ones once carrying him across treacherous fields of battle. But at least he was clean, he thought, his hair tamed, his beard trimmed. A far cry from the man he'd once been but at least he was presentable; presentable enough to begin the search for his son.

Not knowing where else to begin, Nick spent the next few days wandering the streets of Charleston. Once he thought he saw them, the woman and the little boy. But before he could close the distance between them, they had disappeared. The Tory bullet still harbored in his leg rebelled against the constant activity. Nick's limp became more pronounced; he was forced to rest more frequently, lowering himself to the curb until the pain subsided. He was hunched upon the curb, massaging his throbbing muscles, when he saw them the second time, entering Abbey's Mercantile Establishment.

Painfully struggling to his feet, he quickly hobbled across the street to the shop's entrance. The doorknob was in his eager grasp when he hesitated. *Careful*, he warned himself. *Don't frighten them or they'll run away, as they did before.* Slowly, Nick pushed the door inward. The woman stood at the counter, the little boy beside her. He glanced up as Nick entered. His eyes, wide with curiosity, reflected no fear. *Maybe he doesn't recognize me as the filthy man on the street*, Nick thought hopefully.

Palms moist, throat dry, Nick limped toward the two. "Excuse me," he began.

The woman turned her face stern with an intended rebuff.

"Please, I mean you no harm," Nick hurried on. "I was wondering ... I thought ..." He paused; the woman's expression was growing hostile. He took a deep breath. "I ... my name is Nicholas Brisky," he blurted.

The woman stared at him blankly for a moment, then her eyes widened; her mouth shaped itself into a circle of surprise. "Nicholas?" she gasped. "Nicholas Brisky?"

"My wife, Elisa, she died of the fever. I was at war." Fearful of rejection, Nick's words tumbled from his mouth, like frightened sheep. "My son, they said he was taken, by neighbors ..."

"Elisa! Nicholas! Oh, my dear God." The woman glanced quickly at the youngster clinging to her skirts. "We thought you were dead."

* * * *

Victorine Boushey and her husband opened their home to Nick, hoping the reunion with his son would restore his health. Little Nicholas spent many hours at his father's knee, listening to tales of the journey from France, the horror of years at war against the British, the devastating death of his beloved Charles. These stories, recorded in his father's journal were stories little Nicholas would never forget; stories he would later retell to his own children.

In spite of the emotional healing resulting from the reunion with his son, the elder Nick's physical health did not improve. He soon joined his Charles in death leaving little Nicholas II an orphan at the age of seven.

NICHOLAS II
1775–1827

Chapter 7

▼

Sixteen-year-old Nick ran his fingers along the porch banister, testing the wood's rough surface for splinters. He wanted to be certain all was in good repair. He gazed along the familiar row of majestic oak trees lining the narrow street in front of the house. Evening fireflies played hide and seek among their lacey moss-draped branches. The fragrance of honeysuckle hung heavy in the humid South Carolina air. This was Nick's home, the only home he'd known the past eleven years.

Yet, tomorrow, he would face Aunt Victorine with his decision to leave.

It hadn't been an easy decision to make but he knew it was the right one. It was time he made his own way in the world. He was sure it was what his father would have expected of him.

Nick's memory of his father was a vague one with only shadowy recollections of a tall, somber, dark-haired man. He was unaware how closely her resembled that man at whose knee he'd heard frightening tales of a bitter war, the tragic death of his mother, the terrifying burning of their homestead cabin. Those tales, all recorded in his father's journal, were Nick's only knowledge of his past. He'd been told it was neighbors, people he now knew as Aunt Victorine and Uncle Louis, who, during an Iroquois Indian attack on their settlement, snatched Nick from his cradle as they fled to the safety of the colonies.

A sudden moment of indecision formed a lump in Nick's throat as he thought of his surrogate family. Treated as one of their own, Nick had known a happy, secure childhood. The year was 1780 when his "uncle" Louis joined the fight against the British in their attempt to seize Sullivan's Island. During the ensuing battle at Fort Sumpter, Louis lost his life. Being the oldest boy in the household, it fell to Nick to assume the position as man of the family. He dutifully accepted that responsibility, until now.

He stepped down from the porch into the dew-covered grass letting his feet take him where they chose while his mind wrestled, once again, with his decision. Aunt Victorine was well-established, a sought-after seamstress in the town of Charleston now, he rationalized. Her son, Jeremy, soon to turn thirteen, was old enough to assume 'head of the family' duties. Nick would turn seventeen his next birthday. Yes, he concluded. His decision was the right one. It was time for him to be on his own.

*　　*　　*　　*

Leaning against the doorjamb, Nick quietly studied the woman seated at the sewing machine. Her head bent low over the clacking apparatus, she was unaware of Nick's presence. Gnarled fingers methodically fed folds of heavy blue serge beneath the dancing needle. Tired lines tugged at the corners of her mouth, yet graying strands of hair at her temple somehow softened the wrinkles framing her eyes.

For a moment, Nick felt his determination waver. "Aunt Victorine." He could hear the uncertainty in his own voice.

The woman at the sewing machine lifted her foot from its treadle. Her stilled hand resting upon the twilled fabric, she glanced up, a patient smile on her lips. "Yes, Nicholas, what is it?"

Taking a deep breath to fortify his courage, Nick forced carefully memorized words from his reluctant lips. "Aunt Victorine, I've been thinking. Maybe it's time for me to leave here, time I was out on my own. Jeremy is old enough now to take his place as head of the family." He hesitated, apprehension stilling his voice as he awaited the response from his surrogate mother.

A hint of sadness flitted across the woman's face but the smile never left her lips. She sat back, folding her chapped hands in her lap. "I've been expecting this, Nicholas," she sighed. "Actually, I'm surprised it hasn't come sooner. Of course, it's what you must do. Just what are your plans, where will you go?"

"I could probably hire on as a farmhand. I heard talk in town that Mr. Williamson down off Concord Road is needing extra help." Nick paused. "Will you be okay Aunt Victorine?"

"Yes, of course, Nick. Go, if you must. You have my blessing."

* * * *

Nineteen-year-old Nick, uncertainty nibbling at the edge of his resolve, stared at the intimidating white mansion rising before him. Was this plan, after all, a feasible one? Should he have quit his job as farm hand for Mr. Williamson? Nick thoughts scrambled back over the past two years. He'd learned a great deal about farming from his employer but saw little future in working merely for room and board. He recalled his last meeting with Mr. Williamson; the man's graciousness and understanding when he learned of Nick's plan to move on.

"You ought to look up Mr. Merck." Mr. Williamson laid a friendly hand upon Nick's shoulder. "He owns a big cotton plantation west of here. I hear he's wanting to rent out some of his land."

"Thank you, Sir, but as you know, I have no money to pay rent."

"Could be you might be able to work something out with him," Nick's former employer suggested. "It's worth checking into. You just never know."

The directions he'd received from Mr. Williamson brought Nick to where he now stood, waging battle with his inner doubts. The intimidating two-story structure before him clearly bespoke of the owner's wealth. White magnolia bushes leaned heavily upon an arbor arching above the walkway, their overwhelming fragrance hanging heavy in the afternoon air. Huge pillars supported a roof above the grand veranda stretching across the front of the house. Bouganvillia clung possessively to accommodating trellises, their cascade of purple blossoms screening out the heat of a relentless sun. A wicker settee and two matching rockers beckoned invitingly from the cool shadows.

Squaring his shoulders, Nick sucked in a lung full of humid air, hoping it might strengthen the sagging backbone of his courage. Slowly ascending the wide, white steps, Nick paused before the massive double oak doors, his palms grown moist with apprehension. Raising his hand, he rapped firmly upon the hard, grainy wood. In less than an instant, the door opened and Nick found himself facing the questioning gaze of a middle-aged, dark-skinned man.

"Yessuh?" the black man addressed him.

"Ah, Mr. Merck," Nick began nervously. "I ... I'm here to speak with Mr. Merck ... about a job ...?"

"Yessuh," came the obedient reply. "You-all can jus' wait right here while I go fetch Massah Merck."

It was only a matter of moments before the black-skinned servant reappeared. "Massah Merck, he say you-all should wait here. He say he be coming right out." With that, he turned away leaving Nick standing alone in the open doorway.

Nick was debating whether he might be expected to stand where he was or if he might seat himself in one of the wicker rockers when a gentleman appeared at his elbow. A wiry-haired man of advanced years, he towered above Nick, his white hair nearly brushing the top of the door frame. The leanness of his body accentuated his height.

"I'm Mr. Merck." There was no hint of friendliness in the harsh voice. "How can I help you?"

Nick grasped the hard bony hand extended toward him. "Brisky, Nicholas Brisky," he responded quickly. "I was told you might be looking for farm help."

"Well, you been told wrong." The bronzed, weathered face remained unsmiling. "I ain't lookin' for farm hands."

"I'm sorry," Nick stammered. "I ... I thought ..."

The older man's words crowded rudely past Nick's apology. "What I'm looking for is sharecroppers."

Nick's eyebrows arched. "Sharecroppers?"

"I'm willing to rent you a piece of my land," the landowner went on. "They'll be a house on it for you and your family." He paused. "You married? Got a family?"

Nick shook his head.

"No matter. Anyways, I give you the first year's seed. You plant, raise your own cotton, hire your own help. At harvest time, you pay me for the seed I gave you, plus rent for the house and land. Whatever is left over gets divided between you and me. You get half if the crop is good, less if it ain't. Mr. Merck lifted his chin, assessing Nick through narrowed eyes. "You interested?"

Nick could scarcely believe his ears. It was the perfect solution for him "Oh, yes, yes Sir," he replied quickly. "I'm interested."

* * * *

It was on his monthly visit to the mansion to present Mr. Merck with his tally sheets when Nick first set eyes upon Mr. Merck's daughter. As he approached the wide steps to the veranda, he caught sight of a young woman moving about the rose garden to the left of the mansion. In her gown of butter yellow tulle, a flower-filled basket on her arm, Nick decided the lovely maiden offered unfair competition to the colorful garden surrounding her. Apparently hearing his step upon the gravel walkway, she glanced up. Although a wide-brimmed sun hat shaded her face, the afternoon heat had flushed her skin and tendrils of light brown hair clung to her damp cheeks. Nick felt his breath catch in his throat as he stared into a pair of startled gray eyes; saw the slight smile flit across the woman's lips before she turned and bent again to her task.

Nick would later wonder how long he stood there as if rooted to the pathway before he regained his composure and stumbled toward the huge oak doors. Anxiously, he hurried through the presentation of his tallies, hoping to catch sight again of the young lady who had so captivated his fancy. He was to know disappointment for when he left the house, she was no longer in the garden.

In the days that followed, Nick was unable to get her out of his mind; those eyes, the enchanting smile, her delicate beauty would fill his dreams and haunt his waking hours.

Chapter 8

Nick hurried toward the scant shelter of the lean-to. Once inside, he arched his aching back against the brace of his hands. Only a moment before, he'd been swatting at pesky flies buzzing about his head when the storm had erupted. Fascinated as always by these unpredictable tempests, Nick watched as lightning, seeming to explode from the earth, joined land and sky, surrounded the lean-to, drawing Nick into the center of its short-lived fury.

Concern tugged at Nick's dark brows as his hazel-green eyes nervously scanned his carefully cultivated fields. Fibrous puffs already bursting from their bolls, rows of cotton plants bowed their little white heads beneath the onslaught of pelting rain. Impatient for the harvest beginning as early as next week, Nick's uneasiness grew with each possible endangerment to his crop. This year's yield promised to be a good one, and with what he'd learned during this growing season, next year should be even better.

Once again a frown drew those dark brows together. Rain wasn't the only thing feeding his anxiety. Still fresh in his mind was the conversation he'd had last week with Jesse Morgan, a neighboring farmer. There were the boll weevils, rust and leaf worm, Jesse had informed him, all threats to the cotton farmer.

"Root rot is probably the worst," was Jesse's warning. "Your soil is clean, probably 'cause it's lain fallow for the past two years. But once it's infected ..." Jesse shook his head. "Well, that's about it. You might as well figure on rotating your crop with barley or corn until you get rid of the infestation."

The uneasiness aroused by Jesse's words had remained with Nick all week. Was there something he should be doing to ward off such contamination, he wondered? He had no problem with alternating crops; his experience as a farm hand had familiarized him with grain growing. But, how would that affect his sharecropping contract? He decided it best if he had a talk with Mr. Merck.

Stepping from his shelter, Nick glanced toward the big house on the hill, its white pillars barely visible through the screen of large oak trees surrounding it. As usual, the mere sight of it brought forth an image of the young woman he'd seen but once in the past several months. Had she been tending her roses when the storm surprised her, he wondered? Did she seek shelter upon the veranda and watch the storm as he had? A chilling gust of loneliness swept through his him, leaving an aching emptiness in its wake.

Now, Nick decided, might just be a good time to talk to Mr. Merck about boll weevils and root rot.

* * * *

Wet magnolia blossoms drooped from the arbor; their fragrance, teased by the rain, saturated the afternoon air. Slowing his steps as he advanced along the pathway, Nick, as he was wont to do on these visits, glanced hopefully toward the rose garden. Disappointment greeted him once again. Water-drenched flower buds, nodding sluggishly from dripping bushes, were its only occupants. Suppressing a sigh, Nick ascended the wide steps and tapped firmly upon the oaken door panel. Disappointment turned into disbelief as the door swung open and standing on the threshold was the lovely creature who had laid claim to all his waking thoughts. He opened his lips to speak, but the words clung stubbornly to the roof of his mouth.

"Good afternoon, Mr. Brisky." Her voice was as soft and sweet as Nick had imagined it to be. "I suspect you are here to see my father."

"Yes. Yes, I am," Nick stammered. "Is he ... I mean, may I ...?"

"I'm sorry." Her smile sent excited shivers leapfrogging up Nick's spine. "My father is not here right now."

"Forgive me for having troubled you," Nick apologized, quickly backing toward the steps. "I'll just come back later." His departure was unexpectedly interrupted by her next words.

"He should be back soon, if you'd care to wait."

Nick's heart ricocheted against his chest. "Yes," he managed. "Yes, I can wait."

This time, the gray eyes reflected the shy smile tugging at the corners of her mouth. "You can wait here," she suggested, motioning toward one wicker rocker. "I'll have Bella fix some lemonade." She paused in the doorway. "It's always so stifling after the rain," she added, as if to justify the impetuosity of her offer.

Nick had barely seated himself before his young hostess returned carrying the tray of refreshments. He was startled to note the tray held not one, but two tall glasses of the proffered beverage. There was no time to dwell upon the implication as Nick realized the young woman was not alone. Accompanying her was an older, stern-faced woman, her gray hair smoothed back into a tidy bun at the nape of her neck. Nick rose hastily to his feet.

"Mr. Brisky." It was the young woman who addressed him. "This is my mother, Mrs. Merck. Mother, this is Mr. Brisky who is farming the north fields for Father."

Nick dipped his head in acknowledgement. "My pleasure, Ma'am."

Nearly as tall and gaunt as her husband, Mrs. Merck eyed Nick with the same cold, lack of friendliness, her penetrating gray eyes openly assessing him. "I understand you wish to see my husband." She didn't wait for a reply but continued. "I believe my daughter has informed you Mr. Merck is away. However, you may take your leisure here on the veranda until he returns." She turned to the young woman beside her. "Elisabeth, you will see to the comfort of our guest." With that, she disappeared into the house.

To Nick's delight, the young Miss Merck made no move to leave, but, placing the tray on a small table between them, settled herself into the opposite wicker rocker. It was of no surprise to Nick, however, when, a moment later, an amply endowed, dark-skinned woman, who Nick guessed to be Bella, appeared at the end of the veranda, plopping herself into a straight-backed chair positioned there. While fulfilling her secondary roll as chaperone, she silently set about stringing and snapping the colander full of fresh green beans she held in her lap.

Nick studied the droplets of moisture slowly tracing a path down the outside of his frost-covered glass. "This is most kind of you, Miss Merck," he began awkwardly, then hesitated.

"Elisabeth," his young companion was silently mouthing, her gray eyes twinkling.

A grin played across Nick's face as he stole a sidelong glance toward their chaperone.

"This is most kind of you," he repeated, lowering his voice. "Elisabeth," he whispered, savoring the sweetness of her name upon his lips.

The next hour passed with Elisabeth brazenly questioning her guest about the events in his life bringing him to Charleston: Nick answering those questions with an ease he would not have expected. All too soon, Mrs. Merck appeared in the doorway.

"Mr. Merck is home." Her abrupt announcement was directed at Nick. "He will join you shortly." Then, "You will come inside now, Elisabeth," she instructed her daughter.

As Elisabeth stood to obey her mother, Nick rose to his feet. His eyes traveled to the end of the veranda where the black woman, the colander of vegetables balanced precariously on her lap, dozed peacefully. "I've enjoyed this afternoon," he murmured to his young hostess. "May we talk again?"

Darting a furtive glance toward Mrs. Merck's retreating figure, Elisabeth turned back to Nick. Her gray eyes twinkling, a timid smile upon her lips, she nodded quickly before scurrying across the threshold to join her mother.

* * * *

There were still two weeks before the monthly presentation of his tally sheets would provide an excuse for Nick to revisit the young lady who'd stolen his heart. Time crawled by, Nick's only salvation the memory of those unforgettable moments they'd spent on the veranda. Patience not being Nick's strong suit, his mind was made up when finally, at month's end, he approached the white-pillared mansion on the hill.

He hurried up the pathway to the veranda, glancing hopefully, as always, toward the carefully tended garden of roses. His heart dropped a beat, his breath snagged in his throat. There as he had first seen her was Elisabeth, this time wearing a summery gown of lavender, the wide brim of her matching bonnet shading her face. She had seen his approach and, a welcoming smile brightening her face, she moved toward him, picking her way carefully through bud-laden bushes.

"Good morning, Mr. Brisky." She stood next to him now, a slight flush of pink tingeing her cheeks. "My father is waiting for you in the study. I'll tell him you are here."

Struggling to recapture his own power of speech, Nick cringed at the gravelly sound escaping his throat. "Good morning, Miss ..." A gentle lift of her eyebrow brought a crooked smile to Nick's own lips. "Elisabeth," he added softly. "Good morning, Elisabeth. Yes, thank you, please tell your father I am here."

He watched as she started up the path ahead but suddenly, the emotions building inside him the past two weeks could no longer be contained. "Elisabeth," he blurted. She turned, curiosity widening her eyes. "Elisabeth," Nick hurried on. "I ... I'd like to ask your father's permission to call upon you from time to time." Uncertainty subdued his voice. "I mean ... if that pleases you."

A shy smile crept across her lips. "That would please me ... Nicholas," she whispered. "That would please me, very much."

* * * *

Monday through Saturday found Nick tending his cotton crop, inspecting the bursting bolls, overseeing the laborers he hired for harvest time. Sundays were reserved for Elisabeth. Seated together upon the big pillared veranda, they whiled away the warm afternoons. Under the watchful eye of Bella, they soon learned their chaperone was wont to doze as the sun grew warm. It was then they could hold hands, and sometimes, even steal a kiss or two.

Harvest time was over; the cotton baled and sent to market. It had been a profitable year. Even after settling accounts with Mr. Merck, Nick's share had been a gainful one. Thus encouraged, he decided now would be a good time to approach his landlord and request his daughter's hand in marriage.

Chapter 9

Nick received no quarter from Mr. Merck, nor did he expect any, simply because he was married to the man's daughter. Nick continued his status as sharecropper, residing in the small frame house originally provided him. Elisabeth, as well, accepted this absence of favoritism without question. Although far less palatial than the surroundings she'd been accustomed to, she set about turning the bleakness of their living quarters into a comfortable home for herself and her new husband.

Before the year was out, their first child, Polly, was born. With gentle gray eyes twinkling above soft, rosy cheeks and her happy, affectionate disposition, she was a delightful image of her mother. Polly had scarcely begun to teethe when a second daughter, Peggy, arrived. A lush crown of dark hair sprouting above a pair of brooding, hazel green eyes, she was the exact opposite of her blonde, outgoing sister, definitely her father's daughter.

Although some adjustments were deemed necessary, for the time being, the little two-bedroom house provided comfortable space for Nick's family. But with the discovery Elisabeth was again with child came the need to face the inadequacy of their living quarters.

"Perhaps I could speak to Father about providing us a larger house," Elisabeth suggested. "I'm sure he'll understand our need for more room."

Nick's replay had been emphatic. "No! I will care for my own. Our crops are doing well. We will manage this by ourselves."

Setting himself to the task, Nick succeeded in adding two more bedrooms to the limited space of the "share cropper" cabin before the baby, a boy, was delivered. Unfortunately, the child was not strong. In a matter of weeks, he took sick and died. As devastated as Nick was over the loss of their son, he was more concerned about Elisabeth. The child's death affected her, not only physically, but emotionally as well. She slipped into a deep depression. Despite his efforts, nothing Nick said or did could rouse her. In desperation, he reluctantly sought the advice of Elisabeth's mother.

"I don't know how to help her," he confessed to his mother-in-law. "She takes good care of Polly and Peggy but seems to have no interest in anything else. Somehow, I think she blames herself for the baby's death."

A stern, impassive Mrs. Merck displayed little sympathy for her daughter's weakness. "It's not our place to question God's will." Her lips stretched into a thin line of disapproval. "She'll just have to get over it. Maybe it's another child she needs. With a new baby to care for, she'll have less time for her self-pity."

Angry, frustrated, Nick returned home to spend the next few months patiently enduring his wife's unpredictable moods. Hoping to revive her usual interest in gardening, he tilled a six by six plot of ground alongside the cabin, then presented her with flower seeds gathered from helpful neighbors.

From those same concerned friends, he was able to provide enough brightly colored gingham for long-postponed window curtains. But all his efforts to rouse Elizabeth from her apathy proved futile. It wasn't until late August when she became pregnant with their third daughter Katy, that, as Mrs. Merck had predicted, her spirits rose and once again she was Nick's lovely Elisabeth.

With the success of each yearly crop, their security grew, along with the size of their family. They were elated upon the arrival of a son, John. A few years later, little Elisabeth joined the family. While labors were demanding, blessings were many.

But then came the year of the boll weevil.

"Looks like most of the your cotton plants have been invaded." Mr. Merck shook his head, crushing the diseased white ball between his fingers. "Might as well tear them all out. The whole field'll be infected before long."

"What about the new crop, when can I start planting again?"

"Best to give the soil a rest until you're sure it's clean."

"What do I do, then? I can't afford to leave the land fallow."

"Grain is your best bet," Nick's father-in-law suggested. "Not as profitable but, as I see it, you don't have a lot of choice."

That was the year Nick replanted his cotton fields with a barley crop. It was a sturdier crop but, as Mr. Merck had warned, not as profitable. That was also the year Elisabeth gave birth to yet another child, this one stillborn.

It concerned Nick when Elisabeth did not recover quickly from this delivery; seemed slow in regaining her usual energy. While their daughters were now old enough to assume many of the household duties, they knew nothing of how to deal with the deep depression their mother had once again slipped into.

"She hardly talks to us at all," Polly confided to Nick. "Some days, she spends most of the time in her bedroom and I can hear her crying ... a lot."

As before, Elisabeth became obsessed with the need to replace the child she'd lost. Yet, several years passed before Elisabeth was with child again. Although fearful as to whether she had fully recuperated from the last childbirth, it was Nick's hope his wife would, as before, regain her enthusiasm for life. But the pregnancy did not go well. During the final term months, she was confined to her bed. It was Bella's sister Mattie, midwife at the birth of all Elisabeth's children, who tended to the expectant mother. Each time she visited Elisabeth's bedside, Mattie came away shaking her head, her dark, round face scrunched into a worried frown, her pursed lips emitting soft, clucking sounds of doom.

At long last, the baby boy, Nicholas, was born. But it was to be another bittersweet, turning point in Nick's life, for the birth of this son would result in the death of his wife.

* * * *

Seated on the edge of the bed he and Elisabeth had once shared, Nick stared blankly at the paper clutched in his hands. It was the last will and testament of his father-in-law, John B. Merck, gone now these past five years. Sorting through his deceased wife's belongings, Nick had discovered the document in Elisabeth's sewing basket, tucked away beneath scraps of gingham. His eyes slid over the words

"I give and recommend my Soul in the hand of Almighty god," it began. "And as *Such worldly estate, I give and devise and bequeath to my daughter Elisabeth, wife of Nicholas Brisky, One hundred Acres of land."* Nick blinked as the erratically worded phrases blurred before him. *"So God order my plow, should be worked or planted by a Cropper,"* the missive continued, *"than shall the said Nicholas Brisky be clear of it for such time it is plowed by another Cropper."*

Nick felt the shock in the pit of his stomach. It was a moment before he could refocus his eyes upon the lines that followed. *"Money which is to be paid out of the Land Shall be paid to their children."* Wearily, Nick drew his hand across his eyes, pushing back the tears of despair threatening to form there. He knew properties were often willed directly to children instead of the spouse of the deceased. Yet, he had never considered Elisabeth might precede him in death. Again, Nick directed his attention to the directive in his hand. *"Nicholas Brisky shall be clear of it for such time."* With a sigh, he dropped the papers onto the quilted coverlet. Absently, he massaged the ache in his leg, an ache that had grown progressively worse with the passing years. Pitchfork bearing demons of arthritis had colonized within his joints and would give him no peace. It was becoming more difficult for his body to perform the demands he made upon it.

His thoughts turned to his daughters gathered in the next room. Polly, Peggy, Katy, all married now, home for their mother's funeral. They'd be leaving soon, returning to homes of their own. Since each of them was well provided for, there could be no question but that Elisabeth's hundred acres would go to their sons, John and Nicholas.

But what about now, what about little Elisabeth and baby Nicholas? How will I care for them? Arthritic knees rebelled as Nick struggled painfully to his feet. Forcing one foot after the other, he moved toward the unpleasant task of sharing the contents of this last will and testament of one John B. Merck.

* * * *

Aching in both body and spirit, Nick had no energy to argue with the decisions handed down by his daughters. With the experience John had received working the fields with his father, it seemed feasible to his sisters he would soon be able to run the plantation on his own. Until that time, Elizabeth's sister, Philipine, and her husband, living in the big house left to them when the older Mercks passed on, agreed to help John tend the crops. Little Elisabeth would live with Peggy and help her with the family she was now starting. Nicholas III would stay with Polly until he was old enough to make a decision on his share of the hundred acres.

A disheartened, ailing Nick would spend the next few years living with one daughter, and then another, while his health continued to decline. Nicholas III was not yet seven years old when his father died leaving him his most priceless possession, the journalized stories written by Nicholas I.

NICHOLAS III
1810–1863

Chapter 10

▼

"Lawdy, Lawdy. Seem like dem young 'uns ain't neva' gonna' grow up." A throaty chuckle bubbled inside Bertha's ample bosom, finally escaping through the white crescent of a smile slashing its way across her dark, round face.

As if to confirm her observation, a mischievous giggle escaped from the drawing room where Master Nicholas III and his young wife, Aletha, were engaged in one of their often-played children's games. This time, it was hide and seek. The loud "Aha!" erupting from beyond the paneled doors was followed by a gleeful shriek as the seeker discovered his prey. The patter of stocking feet was heard as the chase began.

Shaking her head in resignation, Bertha shuffled through the breezeway connecting the kitchen to the main living quarters. Lifting a water pail from the counter, she pushed open the back door and headed down the short path leading to the well. "Lawd, dey's jes' babes demselves," she muttered softly. "Jes' don' seem right dem 'spectin' a young-un of dey own."

* * * *

Nicholas III had been a defiant young lad of fourteen when chafing beneath her heavy ruling hand, he had left the home of his older sister, Polly, and set out on his own. Having forfeited his education and having little knowledge of anything other than farming, he made his way doing odd jobs, usually settling for little more than room and board for his labors. He was seventeen when, for the usual room and board plus fifty cents, he hired on at the Meadows plantation as farm hand. His room consisted of a cot in the stable where warm animal smells and the snorting of restless horses accompanied his sleeping hours. He took his meals in the kitchen with the household servants.

One of his chores was to trim the honeysuckle bushes growing alongside the main house. This morning as he snipped and clipped at the prolific branches, the unmistakable plinking sound of a piano drifted from the parlor window. He could not resist the urge to peek past the foliage covering the partially open portal. There, seated at a stately upright piano was the loveliest creature he'd ever seen. Chestnut brown hair cascaded across her shoulders and down her back, its dark tendrils curling moistly about her face. Dainty fingers coaxed notes from the rows of off-white and jet-black keys. Though the notes brought forth were monotonous and repetitious, to Nick the music was no less beautiful than that of angels.

Sensing his presence, the young lady glanced up. Nick found himself gazing into a pair of inquisitive brown eyes. He witnessed the sudden flushing of her cheeks, heard her fingers stumble upon the practice routine, a discordant note interrupting the exercise.

"Aletha!" A sharp reprimand reached from a room beyond.

"Yes, Mama," came the girl's dutiful response. Quickly, she lowered her eyes but not before a shy smile danced impishly across her lips.

Nick could not deny his need to see her again. Visions of her drifted through his dreams each night while his days were filled with hopes of a chance meeting with her. He had no way of knowing the young thirteen-year-old Aletha shared those same yearnings. It was she who decided to make the seemingly improbable, happen.

A casual trip to the stable to visit her favorite horse coincided with Nick's morning chore of mucking out the stalls. Nick suddenly became painfully aware of his unkempt appearance; the uncombed disaster of his sleep-tangled hair, the unshaven soft fuzz of an adolescent's beard darkening his jaw, arms and leg stricken with an awkward lack of co-ordination. The young lady took no notice of him, her sweet words being for the mare alone. Miserably mute, Nick watched as, with a gentle pat to the mare's neck, the lovely object of his dreams turned to leave the barn. At the doorway, she paused, glancing across the distance between them.

"Good morning." The sweet sound of her voice sent shivers up Nick's spine. "Would you mind grooming the mare for me today? I have to attend a piano recital."

"Sure, sure," Nick faltered. "I can do that."

Still, the young lady made no move to leave. "My name is Aletha," she offered, her voice barely audible.

Sandpaper dryness invaded Nick's throat. "Nick," he croaked. "I'm Nick …" Then, into the silence that followed, "You play the piano real nice."

Aletha's cheeks reddened. Her shy "thank you" interrupted by an embarrassed giggle bubbling from her lips, she whirled and dashed from the barn, Nick's eyes never leaving her enchanting image as she skipped happily toward the main house.

Their casual though contrived meetings became frequent. Their youthful passion, once unleashed, thus fueled, became difficult to contain. They became reckless, giving little thought to the possibility of detection.

"Meet me behind the woodshed after supper," Aletha whispered when, on another day, she left the barn following a fruitless search for a supposedly lost kitten.

Anticipation having absconded with his appetite, Nick was at the appointed rendezvous long before Aletha. As usual, love filled his heart at the sight of her.

"I was afraid something had happened and you weren't going to make it," he confessed.

Mock dismay clouded Aletha's face. "Do you really believe anything could keep me away," she chided.

Then, to his surprise, she raised herself onto her tiptoes and planted a warm kiss upon his lips. Awkwardly reaching out to draw her to him, he glanced over the top of her head just as Mr. Meadows rounded the corner of the woodshed

Though the anger in Mr. Meadow's eyes was nothing short of murderous, his words were few. "Get back to the house, young lady," he ordered Aletha. He waited until his frightened daughter had scurried past him before turning upon Nick. It was a moment before he spoke again, the taut muscles of his jaw betraying an effort to control his anger. "As for you, Nicholas Brisky ..."

"You don't understand, Mr. Meadows. Aletha and I ..."

"No, YOU don't understand. I want you off my property by sun down"

Chapter 11

A misty rainbow circled the moon, the single star entrapped within its halo promising rain in as many days. Cautiously, Nick slipped from the sheltering growth of trailing wisteria where he'd sought refuge until the departing sun gave way to darkness. Plucking a pebble from the walkway at his feet, he tossed it toward the upstairs window he knew to be Aletha's. The white lace curtain fluttered, then was still. Minutes became eternities as he waited until, suddenly, she was at his side. He gathered her into his eager arms.

"Oh, Nick. I was so afraid you wouldn't come back after this afternoon … after Father …" He could hear the tears in her voice.

"Aletha, you know I couldn't leave without seeing you." He gently brushed rough fingers over her weep-reddened eyes. "I was afraid you wouldn't be able to get out of the house."

"Father locked me in my room but he forgot about the opening in my closet that leads to the back stairway. Oh, Nick, what are we going to do?"

Nick's arms tightened about his love. "Come away with me, Aletha," he whispered into her hair. "I've got some land left to me by my grandfather," he hurried on. "I'll sell it. We can start a new life somewhere else, away from here."

"Oh, yes, Nick." Aletha snuggled deeper into Nick's embrace. "Yes! Yes! Yes!"

* * * *

John stared at the couple standing before him, the gangly young man who was his brother, the petite young girl beside him. "Are you sure this is what you want to do, Nick? Half this plantation is yours, you know," he argued. "It's been a profitable business these past years, good crops, good market. You could move back here, we could share the plantation, work it together."

Nick shook his head. "No, John. I want to leave Carolina. I'm going to sell my share, to you or anyone who wants to buy it."

It was obvious his younger brother had made up his mind. "Very well, Nick," John sighed. "Come into my office. We'll draw up the papers."

His inheritance money in his pocket, Nick was eager to leave the unhappy memories of Charleston behind. It was shortly before dawn the following morning when Nick and Aletha joined John aboard his horse-drawn carriage. Nick's brother had agreed to help them find their way to the new stagecoach station located several miles north of the plantation.

"Some fellow in Virginia has started up a stagecoach line to carry overland mail," John had informed Nick the night before. "The coach swings south through the Carolinas before heading on to Georgia. Maybe its because the company is privately owned but I've heard the driver sometimes, for a fee, will take on passengers heading west."

Nick and Aletha considered themselves fortunate to finally overcome the driver's reluctance to grant passage to two so-young travelers. Later, they would question that good fortune as they endured the rough bone-bruising journey across rugged mountain passes of the Appalachians, their coach bouncing and jostling over the bumpy, corduroy-like terrain. All-too-short respites at all-too-few stagecoach inns along the way brought little relief to their weary, aching bodies. Although short of their destination, they were grateful when they were at last deposited at LaFayette, Georgia, the final stop.

"The first thing we'll do is buy a horse and wagon," Nick decided. "Then we'll pick up supplies before we head cross the border into Alabama." He glanced down at Aletha, anticipating her affirmative response. She remained silent, her eyes mirroring reproof. The frown of consternation tugging at Nick's brow gave way to the twinkle in his own eyes. "You're right," he grinned. "The first thing we'll do is find a justice of the peace.

*   *   *   *

Hands tightly clasped, Nick and Aletha stood in the living room of Theodore Malcom, Justice of the Peace. Only yesterday, he had issued them a marriage license and now, one day later, in accordance with the laws of Georgia, Justice T. Malcom prepared to join them in holy wedlock. The Justice's smiling wife stood beside him, prepared to witness the whispered "I do's" of the young couple. Although the short, sterile ceremony was devoid of all fancy trappings, for Nick and Aletha it would ever remain the most beautiful moment in their lives.

"Where are you young folks headed?" Justice Malcom smiled at the starry-eyed newly-weds standing before him.

Reluctantly, Nick switched his attention to their benefactor. "We're headed for Alabama," he explained. "I have a small inheritance. I intend to invest in a cotton plantation."

The clerk arched an eyebrow. "Do you have any particular property in mind?"

"Well, no. I guess we'll look until we find the place that's just right."

"Hmmm." Justice Malcom tugged thoughtfully at his beard. "I understand there's an abandoned plantation outside Milltown, just across the border. Fellow who owned it pulled the life out of the land then left it. It's lain fallow for about a year now. The soil may have had time to restore itself." He paused, studying the young man's face, intent now with interest. "It would take some work," he suggested. "But it might turn out to be just right for you."

Nick and Aletha exchanged excited smiles. "Thank you, Sir." Nick grasped the hand of the man before him. "Thank you. I'm beholding to you, Sir."

* * * *

His new bride beside him, his heart bursting with joy, Nick slapped the reins against the horse's rump setting the wagon in motion toward Alabama and their new life.

Bouncing their way along rutted roads, they crossed the border into Alabama in search of the "just-right" piece of property. Justice Malcom's directions brought them to the edge of doubt and disappointment. From the seat of their wagon, it was obvious the abandoned plantation had been allowed to fall into a discouraging state of disrepair. None-the-less, they decided to investigate. Climbing down from their vantage point, they chose to disregard the dilapidated two story house and directed their attention to the acreage beyond. Their exploratory stroll brought them unexpectedly into an arroyo concealing a nearly dry riverbed. A lethargic rivulet of water trickled where a once a river had gushed leaving behind a most unusual deposit of river rock. Sparkling shards of colorful quartz glittered and winked at them in the late afternoon sun.

"Oh, Nick!" Aletha gasped. "How beautiful!"

Nick's eyes softened as he watched the glow of rapture transform his young wife's face. "This plantation will be ours," was his sudden announcement. "This rock quarry will belong to us."

With a squeal of delight, Aletha flung herself into her husband's arms. Nick hugged her small frame to him. "Furthermore, my love," he brashly declared, "from these rocks, I'll build you the grandest of fireplaces, the likes of which you've never seen before."

* * * *

Eventually, Nick would keep his promise. But first there was the legal process of acquiring the land. Once all necessary transactions were completed, the land was finally his, but other priorities took over, priorities which would send him halfway across Alabama to the wharves of Mobile. There was no disputing the fact Nick could not restore the neglected fields and operate the plantation without help. While not an advocate of the accepted practice of slavery, Nick grudgingly conceded there was little choice left him. The financial success of his dream was dependent upon the use of unsalaried labor. He set off to the seaport town of Mobile where ships were docking daily, depositing human cargoes to be auctioned off by slave merchants. He wasn't prepared for what he found at the waterfront. The troubling memory would long remain with him, follow him, even into his worst dreams.

Rats scurried underfoot, unheeded amid the chaotic bargaining, poking their inquisitive noses from dark, fetid hiding places. Far worse, for Nick, than the stench of rotting fish was the smell of fear rising from human bodies. Frightened huddles of humanity, eyes wide with terror, dark-skinned bodies glistening with sweat, watched helplessly as their families were callously torn asunder, sold to the highest bidder.

"It was awful, Aletha," he later shared with his wife. "Those poor, wretched people were being treated like ... like cattle." He blinked back the moisture gathering behind his eyelids. "I wanted to bring them all home," he confessed.

Tears welling in her own eyes, Aletha gently massaged her husband's bowed shoulders. "Oh, Nick, how terrible. We must never let that happen here."

Nick gathered Aletha in his arms. Together they vowed none in their servitude would ever suffer such indignity.

The small number of slaves Nick was reluctantly compelled to bring back to Milltown, soon grew to nearly one hundred, but Nick and Aletha never abandoned the promise they'd made to one another. Their compassion, coupled with their exuberant lust for life, endeared the young Master and Mistress to those humans they'd taken into their charge.

* * * *

Once the tiny cotton plants had been snugly tucked into the rejuvenated soil, Nick turned his attention to the building of their home. He selected a high knoll, set back in a thick grove of trees and began construction. When it was completed, the grand edifice would boast of massive white pillars supporting numerous decks surrounding the impressive high, double oaken door entrance. Next, Nick ordered stones carried from the quarry each day until the magnificent fireplace of glittering quartz he'd promised Aletha had been created. It was, indeed, the likes of which had never been seen before. The massive formation took up one entire wall of the spacious living room, huge, sparkling stones rising from floor to ceiling. Carefully selected smaller stones were used to form an arched opening large enough to accommodate the great long-burning fire logs. It was truly a fitting monument of Nick's devotion to his young bride.

Once the house was established, a large orchard soon sprang into being behind it. Beyond, were the cotton fields and housing for his laborers and their families. Not far from the slave quarters, Nick built a large elevated platform. Sturdy pillars supported the cone shaped roof protecting the wooden flooring below. At this grandstand, the slaves gathered each morning to receive the day's instructions and hear important announcements from "the Massuh". Evenings, it became the gathering place where the workers relaxed from the day's labors. Someone provided "comb" music and, from somewhere, a flute even appeared. Ever eager to enter into any festivities, Nick and Aletha frequently joined in, singing and dancing along with their laborers.

* * * *

It was in the spring of 1840. A warm breeze entering through the window opened to the June night did little to appease Nick's anxiety. Restlessly, he paced the hallway outside their bedroom where Aletha bravely endured the agonizing pains of her first childbirth. Night shadows were disappearing into the morning light before, at long last, an exhausted midwife appeared in the doorway. Smiling, she gently placed the small white bundle she carried into Nicks waiting arms.

That morning, Nick appeared before the gathering at the grandstand, a little white bundle cradled in his arms. He stood quietly, for a moment, then lifted the child above his head so that all might see. "This is my son," the grinning young master announced proudly. When the cheering had subsided, he held his son close to him. Gazing into the tiny, red face, he was quiet for a moment. Then, "You shall be called Jasper Newton," he added softly, "for the two friends who once saved my granddaddy's life."

Chapter 12

▼

September 29th, molasses-making day. Nick closed his eyes and, tossing back his head, filled his lungs with the crisp fall air, allowing the tantalizing sounds and smells of autumn to seduce his senses. Pumpkins were turning on the vine, recently harvested beans and peas, drying on great canvasses, would soon pop their shells. Baskets of dried peaches and apples, gathered from the orchards behind the mansion, stood ready for market. Time had come for winter pleasures.

As most of the cotton crop had been gathered, the gin mill and cotton baler were silent today. Their incessant din and dust had given way to the lush smell drifting from a huge vat where sugarcane juices bubbled and boiled, transforming themselves into a honey-like syrup, a delight to send any true Southerner into ecstasy. The mere anticipation of hot biscuits, fresh churned butter and new molasses melting on his tongue set Nick's own juices to salivating.

From his vantage point upon the huge deck, Nick gazed out across the far-reaching expanse of his plantation. Years of prosperity had enabled him to increase its size to nearly one thousand acres. While this created the need to purchase more slaves, Nick continued to honor the promise he and Aletha had made to one another. He made certain slave families remained together, often purchasing a youngster in lieu of a more productive worker in order to avoid the separation of mother and child.

As his estate grew, so did his family. A gentle smile softened Nick's angular features, his thoughts turning to Nancy, an only daughter among their brood of thirteen. As quickly as it arrived, the fleeting smile disappeared. With a twinge of sadness, he recalled the two tiny lads taken from them by Death.

Wresting himself from the futility of such reminiscing, Nick squinted into the late afternoon sun toward where, beyond the scope of his vision, lay the land belonging to his remaining sons. Pride smoothed the frown burrowing across his brow as his thoughts turned to Jasper, Miles, John, Marion, Hollaway, Jesse, George, William, Dudley and little Nicholas IV. The plot of land he'd willed to each of them at the time of their birth would be tilled and cultivated until they were of age. Not only would this provide a place to bring a bride when the time was right, it would also guarantee security for Nick's unborn grandchildren.

Nick turned at the sound of footsteps behind him. An eager twinkle danced into his eyes, a boyish grin stealing across his face. Slipping an arm about her waist, he drew Aletha to him. As always, whenever they were together, the years fell away and they were, once again, teen-aged newly-weds.

"Ah, is it my company you miss, my love," Nick chided, "or rather the lure of 'lasses' brewing in yonder pots that brings you to my side?"

Aletha playfully dug an elbow into Nick's ribs. "I just happen to have already been allowed a taste of Bertha's huckleberry pie," she taunted. "While you were out here coveting that pot of 'lasses', I been helpin' Bertha put together her special six-layer cake."

Nick clutched his stomach in mock pain. "How can you torture me so, woman? I am nearly to expire from my hunger."

"I sincerely doubt that," Aletha giggled. "Anyway, the sweet potatoes and cornbread are done. Soon as Bertha takes the squirrel pie from the oven, she says the feast can begin."

It was early evening when everyone had finally eaten his fill. It was time for the slaves and their families to gather in the big yard in front of the mansion. Once again, comb and paper appeared, along with the mysteriously purveyed flute, to provide music for the round play-dances of the day. It was 8:30 before festivities finally ended; slaves and their families returning to their own respective dwellings, while Nick retired his family into the big house.

Once all were inside, it was time for the nightly ritual. Nick climbed upon a stool to wind the eight-foot grandfather clock standing against the drawing room wall. Once that nightly ritual was completed, chairs were then pulled into a half-circle before the grand fireplace. While the mansion now boasted of many rooms, each with its own fireplace, it was in front of Aletha's granite fireplace where the family always gathered.

After a great deal of bustle amid scraping sounds of chairs being re-positioned, everyone was finally seated. Aletha lifted the family Bible from its place atop the mantle and carried it to where Nick sat in the middle of the semi-circle. The family listened attentively while Nick read the selected chapter, watched as he carefully closed the sacred tome, then bowed their heads for prayer. Although little feet shuffled restlessly and tired bodies shifted in discomfort, Nick stubbornly refused to bring the prayer to a close until its length was no less than what his God deserved.

Life was good for Nick and Aletha. They had a beautiful home, a prosperous plantation, a lovely daughter and healthy sons to carry on the family name. But, an unexpected call to arms was to shatter their complacency, disrupting a world, a lifestyle, they were never to know again. The country's new president was announcing his intention to abolish slavery, the very foundation of Southern prosperity. The South suddenly found itself involved in a civil war between the states. As had their forefathers in France under Napoleon, and in America under General Washington, the sons of the House of Brisky were among the first to answer the call. Six of Nicholas's sons went forth to fight against what they believed to be a threat to their way of life.

* * * *

Nick stood in the doorway of the Brisky mansion, his arm about Aletha. He could feel her slender body tremble against his as they watched three of their sons disappear down the once familiar, now strangely ominous, oak-lined driveway leading into the unknown horrors of war. Jasper, Miles and Jesse, ages 27, 19 and 17, were heading for Camp Watts at Auburn, Alabama where they were mustered into service with the 14th Alabama Regiment, Company D, under a General French.

It was Jasper who sent letters providing Nick and Aletha with sketchy bits of information about their soldier sons, letters they read and reread, huddled together before the great stone fireplace. From these scraps of correspondence, they learned the frightening news of Jasper's near capture while on scouting duty; how he and three others escaped and, wearing enemy clothing, managed to make their way back to their regiment.

"*We ran into Hampton's cavalry.*" The letter explained. "*Through combined efforts, we recaptured our men in about four hours, along with six hundred negro women, buggies, carriages, jewelry and other plunder the Yankies had taken. We sent these spoils back to their owners.*"

Another letter informed them, "*I was at Fort Mahone when Petersburg blew up. It was about 4:00 a.m. and we were but two miles away. At 10:00 a.m. Wright's brigade made the first efforts to recapture the works. They were repulsed by negros. Then Mahone's Virginia Brigade attempted and was repulsed. At 2:00 p.m. Wilcox's Alabama Brigade captured the works using bayonets and clubbing with muskets. I was at Druey's Bluff which was a terrible slaughter.*"

Aletha could only turn her face to sob into Nick's shoulder while he fought to control the stinging moisture gathering behind his own eyes.

On other occasions, the messages they received from Jasper were of a bittersweet nature, filling them with a mixture of parental pride and anxiety.

"*Near Petersburg, at Deep Bottom, the main Federal army was north of a creek when a corps swung around us and had us hemmed in inside the bend of the creek. The Federals were trying to plant their artillery on a little hill overlooking our men. They were driven back and the hillside was strewn with the bodies of dead men, both Rebels and Yankees. The hill was a point of vantage and both sides wanted it. A little captain from Georgia said 'The Yankees are all around us. If they get the hill, we are gone.' He pleaded with his men to go with him to charge the enemy and take the hill. However, the dead and dying* were before our eyes and the men shrunk from what seemed to be sure slaughter.

Then the captain called for volunteers. My chum, Brewster, stepped forward and said, 'Brewster, 14 Alabama, Co. D'. Then my other chum stepped out and said 'Berns, 14 Alabama, Co. D'. I could not stand back like a coward and let my chums go alone so I stepped forward and said, 'Brisky, 14 Alabama, Co. D'. The captain yelled out as tears rolled down his cheeks, 'Are you Georgians going to stand by and let Alabama outdo you?" The captain's regiment rallied. Every man fell in and we took the crest of the hill. We gathered rails from an old house and held the hill until a part of the Longstreet Corps came to reinforce us. We three Bs were commended for our loyalty."

Many weeks passed before they heard from Jasper again. It was during this time word reached Nick and Aletha their son Hollaway had been killed in a battle at Winchester.

Chapter 13

Letters from Jasper grew shorter, further apart. The infrequency of news was all the more disturbing since Nick and Aletha were still coping with the loss of their son, Holloway. A cold fist of fear, wrapped about their hearts, became their daily companion.

"I fought with General Sedgewick in the 8th and 9th Brigade." Four bitter lines from Jasper brought home the gruesome reality of the war. *"I saw General Sedgewick fall from his horse, mortally wounded. A soldier dropped by his side, robbing the body before it had hardly touched the ground."*

Nick and Aletha soon learned plundering was not confined merely to the battlefield. They, as well as their neighbors, were on constant guard against marauders, not only Yankee soldiers but also looting opportunists.

Still, in spite of the dangers, crops needed tending. Today, as usual, Nick, astride his favorite stallion, conducted his daily supervision of the harvest, weaving his way through the rows of cotton. The hot, mid-day sun shimmered across the backs of slaves as they bent to their task, arms glistening with the sweat of labor.

The sudden vibrating sound shattering the humid Alabama afternoon; stilled the pickers' hands, their eyes widening in terror. Chills leapfrogged up Nick's spine as he recognized the unmistakable gong of the cast iron dinner bell. Hung beside the well, its purpose a signal of distress, it now pealed an urgent cry for help.

Nick twisted in his saddle, his eyes probing the distance between himself and the white-pillared house on the hill. Even from this range, he was able to make out the cluster of blue-jacketed figures milling about the mansion's front yard. With a cry of rage, he jerked upon the reins, digging his heels into the stallion's flanks. Giving little thought to his own danger, Nick snatched the rifle from its scabbard, firing warning shots into the air as horse and rider hurtled recklessly across the fields. The band of looters was no more than a cloud of dust when Nick reached the porch. He scarcely noticed Bertha, face frozen in terror, her fingers still clutching the bell rope. Leaping to the ground, Nick bounded up the steps and through the open doors.

"Aletha!" His anxious cries searched frantically through the many-roomed mansion. "Aletha!"

Her soft sobs drew Nick to where his frightened wife crouched in an alcove beneath the grand winding stairway. Little Nicholas IV, aged four, cowered beside her, wild-eyed with fear. Nick knelt quickly beside his wife. "Aletha! Are you all right? Are you hurt?" he demanded.

"Oh, Nick. Oh, Nick. It was so frightening."

Nick gathered her to him, rocking her gently as he cradled her in his arms.

"They ... they took things," she hiccuped into his chest. "Silverware, money from the coin chest ..."

Nick glanced toward his young son whose eyes now brimmed with unrestrained tears.

He slipped his arm around Nicholas' shoulder. "It does not matter," he soothed. "As long as you are both safe."

The very next day, Nick and Aletha buried a box in the floor of the smokehouse. Over the box, they built a bench out of a pine stump, a bench to be used for cutting meat at butchering time. In the back of the stump was a knothole leading through a hollowed out channel into the buried box. Gold and silver coins were dropped through the knothole into the box. Sometimes, even confederate money was added to their stash although the new issue was being circulated within the eleven Confederate States of America in such quantities, it had little value. A barrel of flour cost three hundred confederate dollars, a pair of shoes, one hundred fifty. With the construction of their home made saving bank, Nick and Aletha hoped to protect the family's diminishing savings against both inflation and looters.

*   *   *   *

News from the battlefront drifted to the plantation. A terrible confrontation at Seven Pines followed by the Seven-Day Battle of Richmond took the lives of many young Confederate soldiers, including that of their son Miles. Seventeen-year-old Jesse lost his right hand, and subsequently, his life in the Battle of Norfolk. John, blinded in combat, died in camp during an epidemic of measles. And, still, there had been no word from Jasper.

Their apprehension made Nick and Aletha's days nearly unbearable before, finally, a letter arrived. Jasper was at a medical encampment, wounded in the battle at Marvin Hill, the same battle that took Jesse's life.

"I was shot in the right leg, the bullet lodging between the bones, just below the knee."

A shudder ran through Nick and he stared, with unseeing eyes, at the letter in his hands. The wound described by his son was identical to the one received by his grandfather, Nicholas I, in the Revolutionary War.

Although Nick and Aletha prayed their son would be allowed to come home when released from the hospital, their prayers were not to be answered. Jasper's next letter informed them he was being assigned to serve with General Robert E, Lee. It was during a time of unusually low temperatures, later proving to be one of the severest of winters.

"General Lee is a great soldier, loved by all his men," Jasper wrote. *"Two other soldiers and I were trying to find something to relieve our almost unbearable conditions,"* he went on to confess. *"We were surprised by General Lee whose only reprimand was, 'You are a soldier, not a marauder. Go back to your command.'"*

Nick and Aletha felt no shame at their son's confession. Hardships of their own had robbed them of any judgmental inclinations. Jasper would still be under his command when General Lee surrendered at Appotomax on the 10th day of June, Jasper's birthday.

Unfortunately, Nick's earlier efforts to protect the family's fortune proved fruitless. The legacy he had built was destroyed, his family debilitated. Heartbroken, unable to cope with the terrible losses, Nick joined those of his sons buried in the cemetery behind the mansion.

The afternoon following Nick's funeral, Aletha made many trips from the smokehouse, carrying great aprons full of confederate money into the mansion. There, with tears streaming down her cheeks, she watched the worthless bills turn to ashes in her grand stone fireplace.

NICHOLAS IV
1859–1933

Chapter 14

Nicholas IV was but a toddler when his father, Nicholas III, died of a broken heart. The years that followed the elder Nick's death were filled with hardship and uncertainty. The War-Between-the-States fought primarily on southern soil, left much of the land unfit for crops. This combined with the deprivation of free labor necessary for their affluent lifestyle, forced once wealthy land barons, including the Brisky family, to exist on the meager income from diminished cotton crops coaxed from the ravaged soil.

"I ain't goin' nowheres." Bertha scrunched her plump face into a defiant scowl. As longtime housekeeper and caregiver for the Brisky family, she refused to take advantage of her new freedom. "Who gonna' take care of da missus and dem babies if I leaves?"

Aletha, still wrapped in the arms of grief, brushed away tears of gratitude dampening her cheeks. Unlike Bertha, many of the newly emancipated Brisky slaves chose to strike out on their own. Yet, others, whether out of loyalty or fear of the unknown, chose to remain on the plantation, assuming the Brisky name simply because they had none of their own. These loyal few, tending the dwindling cotton crops, contributed to the survival of the Brisky plantation.

Gazing out into the circle of dark, expectant faces surrounding the weathered platform of the grandstand, Jasper, now the eldest surviving son, thanked his loyal servants the only way he knew how.

"For each of you, there will be a plot of land, to plant and cultivate as your own," he began. "It will belong to you, or your children, for as long as you choose, to do with as you wish."

Silence greeted his proclamation. Slowly, timidly, a murmur of uncertainty tiptoed through the gathering of ex-slaves. As disbelief turned into acceptance, then elation, white smiles of joy slashed across dark faces, erupting, finally, into excited cheers. Eternal loyalty to their one-time masters was established.

Beaten, but not broken, proud Southerners, never conceding to having lost the war, struggled stubbornly to retain the old way of life. But it soon became apparent their ravaged plantation could not support the entire Brisky clan. On his arduous journey to manhood, Nick watched his siblings, one by one, forced to leave the palatial mansion they knew as home. His only sister, Nancy, married and moved on to a life with her new husband. His brother, Marion, took a native Indian princess as his bride, a union taking him into an entirely different colony. Another brother, Dudley, brought a wife to the plantation but chose to leave following her untimely death.

Jasper, married now, clung tenaciously to his plot of land, managing to support his small family by renting out three tenant homes standing between his property and the old mansion. Optimistically, he began construction of a two-story house to replace his smaller home. Before his project was completed, his wife's health began to fail.

"I don't want what happened to Dudley, happening to me," Jasper agonized to Nick.

"I'm taking Ellen to Missouri where she can be close to her own people. Maybe, there, her health will improve."

Before he left, Jasper donated a piece of his land to the city of Milltown for a new schoolhouse. With the help of neighbors, Nick and his brothers erected the building henceforth known as "The Brisky School." Finding a schoolteacher proved to be a bit more of a problem. Their search ended with the arrival of Miss Weeks, a stern-faced, middle-aged schoolmarm from a neighboring community, displaced when marauding soldiers burned her schoolhouse. Unfortunately, there were no funds within Milltown's school district to pay her fee. Parents with more than one child were unable to afford the necessary tuition of four dollars per month for each child.

"I would be willing to solicit the community for more students," argued Miss Weeks. "But I have to be guaranteed living expenses."

Until the required number of students enrolled to insure a satisfactory wage for Miss Weeks, each family agreed to provide her with one month's room and board in their own home.

* * * *

Even the most difficult times fail to dampen the undefeatable enthusiasm of youth. So it was with twenty-three-year-old Nicholas. He labored diligently in the cotton fields all week but on Saturday nights, Nick, along with several companions, made the jaunt south to revel in the nightlife of New Orleans. This city, inhabited by a myriad of diverse nationalities, each clustered in their own ethnic community, offered an unending assortment of entertainment for restless young men. Nick and his friends investigated them all.

Attending an open-to-all celebration in the Irish sector one evening, Nick met Mattie Alice Moore, a winsome young Irish lass. As the festivities progressed, he found himself keenly attracted to this saucy eighteen-year-old. The young lady's family, he was told, driven from Ireland by the 1847 potato famine, hoped to find a better way of life in New Orleans. Nick marveled that the obvious hardships they endured had done little to squelch Mattie's bubbly enthusiasm for life. By the end of the evening, he was totally infatuated with this auburn-haired, green-eyed charmer.

Reluctant to leave, Nick lingered until nearly all the guests had departed and he was, at long last, able to have a private moment with Mattie. "I'd truly like to see you again," he offered. "May I have permission to call upon you?"

"If 'tis permission you need, you'll not be getting it from me," she teased, her nose crinkling above an impish grin, her green eyes sparkling mischievously. "But, should a Johnny Reb have a mind of his own, I'll not be turning the likes of him away from my doorstep."

"Johnny Reb is it?" Nick found himself grinning back at her. Leaning closer, he traced a playful finger over the spattering of freckles dancing across the fragile bridge of her nose. "Very well, then," he retaliated. "I shall call you 'Pug'. And you'll be finding me on your doorstep come Saturday morn."

During that summer, Nick spent the weekdays applying himself to the demands of the plantation, but his weekends were spent in pursuit of the courtship of his adored "Pug." At the end of summer, they were wed and Nick brought Mattie home to the aging Alabama mansion.

Chapter 15

Nick and his new wife had scarcely settled into the old house they now shared with Aletha and Bertha when Nick's brothers, William and George, called him aside. It was a serious-faced William who broke the news.

"Sorry to desert you, Nick, but George and I have been talking it over and, well, we've decided to leave Alabama, try our luck somewhere else." He hurried on, averting his eyes from Nick's ashen face. "There's nothing here anymore, you'll have to admit that, Nick. Bad crops, poor markets, we can't see any future here, for us, or our families." He looked up then, meeting his younger brother's stricken gaze. "You should think about getting out of here, too, Nick. The old South is gone, it will never be the same again."

"When are you leaving? Where ..." Nick swallowed past the lump in his throat. "Where will you go?"

William sighed. "There's another family, the Treadwells, heading for Texas," he divulged. "We're joining them. We'll leave just as soon as everyone is packed and ready."

A few days later, standing at the end of the oak-lined drive, Nick watched as, their possessions packed into covered wagons, the last of his brothers left the Brisky plantation Some time later, Nick received a letter from William informing him his brothers had arrived and settled in Texas. Another letter disclosed that, having learned of land grants being offered by the Northern Pacific Railroad, they'd decided to move on to the Pacific Northwest.

George will be going on up the Yakima River to some place called Leavenworth, William wrote. *I bought one hundred sixty acres in a beautiful little valley, not far from the small town of Cashmere.* The rest of his letter, and those following, were filled with flowing descriptions of his newly discovered paradise. He painted word pictures of tall pines, whispering in a gentle breeze, an abundance of wild game, deep rich black soil, a constant fresh water stream originating at an artesian spring bubbling up at the head of a canyon. *There, at the toe of the mountain, is where I will build my home*, William continued. *I do wish you'd consider joining us, Nick. It's a paradise out here.*

But Nick's attention was upon other issues. For it was during this time their ailing mother, Aletha, joined her husband in the little cemetery behind the mansion. In his grief, Nick wondered if his brothers were right. Perhaps he, too, should leave this dying plantation, start a new life somewhere else.

Shortly after Mattie had given birth to little William, Nick received yet another letter from his brother, a letter bringing terrible news. William's cabin tucked at the foot of the mountain ... destroyed by a snow slide. Erratic, broken sentences filled the letter; words of remorse writhed painfully across its pages. William and his neighbors dug for eight frantic hours searching for survivors. Bell, the baby, and five-year-old Mary, both safe, but Laura, William's wife, and a visiting minister smothered beneath the heavy snow. Guilt tinged the missive Nick held in his hand. It had been William and his neighbor, felling trees above the cabin, who triggered the avalanche.

At that moment, although his heart ached for William, Nick firmly discarded all thoughts of joining his brothers in a land no less cruel than his own.

*   *   *   *

Nick and Mattie struggled to eke a living from the plantation while their family continued to grow in number, bringing them both joy and heartache. The rooms of the old mansion overflowed with the happy sounds of the children; Susan, Nicholas, John, Aletha, Carrie, William. They also sheltered the anguish of sorrow when, Lilly, born in 1889, was taken by the summer sickness before she was a year old. Shortly thereafter, little Nannie arrived, then George, Alvie and Jesse, followed by Guy, Pearl, Mattie and Inez and, finally, the birth of little Thomas rounded out their numbers to sixteen. Even with Lily lost to them there remained fifteen hungry mouths to feed.

Letters from William continued to arrive, now offering to sell his land to Nick. Remarried, starting a new family, William no longer wished to remain in his 'paradise lost.' Nick's life was no better. Markets for his meager cotton crops were becoming more difficult to find. Having enrolled his children in school, he now, after six or eight years of schooling, felt the need to pull them from the educational system to help in the fields.

Adding to his woes was the constant need to beware of wandering tribes of gypsies. Considered irresponsible, immoral, even evil, these bands of drifters were becoming a blight upon the Southland, preying upon landowners for their existence. Any farmer, naïve enough to allow them on his land was rewarded with the loss of not only his prized livestock but also any other valuables left unguarded. Even more frightening, gypsies were known to kidnap young children.

There had been no forewarning, no premonition to prepare him when, as each day after the evening meal, Nick stepped out onto the great pillared veranda. Dusk was his favorite time of day. Arching his tall, lanky frame against the brace of his callused hands, Nick filled his lungs with the warm late afternoon air; let his eyes drink in the comforting expanse of his land. Recovering from the scars of war, it once again exuded the familiar beauty of a tranquil South. Majestic oak trees lined the driveway, lacey curtains of Spanish moss cascading from their branches. Graceful magnolia blossoms dripped from their arbors, filling the air with the sweetness of their fragrance. Nick sighed. *This is my home*, he thought. *This is where I belong. I'll never leave until I no longer have strength to till the soil.*

As his gaze slid across the fields, Nick felt the breath catch in his throat, the muscles of his stomach knot. Above the grassy knoll just beyond the house, a wisp of smoke curled into the air. His searching eyes came to rest upon an ancient, dilapidated wagon; beside it a motley group of gypsies hovered about a cook fire.

"Thieves! Vagabonds!" The words exploded from his lips, shattering the quiet serenity of the soft twilight.

Sometime, during the day, evidently while he'd been occupied in the fields, they had crept, undetected, onto his land. At one time, negro laborers who considered gypsies bad luck would have been the ones to drive them away. Now it was Nick, seething with anger, who strode across the field and into the gypsy camp. He wasted no time in delivering his short, hostile ultimatum.

"You are not welcome here," he snarled. "You will have to move on."

White teeth flashing against his dark skin, their leader smiled disarmingly. "Of course, padrone, it will be as you wish. Ah, but let us rest here for our evening meal. We will be gone by morning."

"I want you gone by nightfall," Nick countered. As he turned on his heel to leave, he noticed an old woman, staring at him from across the bonfire. He hesitated, startled by the hatred he saw glittering in her dark eyes before she looked away. He felt his spine tingle as he strode back to the mansion; knew those eyes followed him every step of the way.

It was Mattie's frightened cry awakening him the following morning. "Nick! There's a gypsy woman down by the well."

Hurrying to her side, Nick peered out the window. His surprise turned to anger when he spied the bedraggled, ragtag old crone he'd seen at the gypsy camp the night before. Leaning against the stone perimeter of the well, three moisture-beaded goat skin water bags lying at her feet, the old woman blatantly sipped from the enameled water dipper intended for family use. Slamming the screen door behind him, Nick quickly covered the distance across the yard.

"What are you doing here?" he demanded. "You were told to be gone by last night."

"You would begrudge a thirsty traveler a small drink from your well?" she whined.

Snatching the dipper from her hand, Nick flung it to the ground. "You have filled your water bags. Take your parasitic band of thieves and leave! Now!"

The old woman was silent for a moment, staring at the enameled vessel lying in the dust at her feet. When she looked up, even a dauntless Nick blanched at the venomous hatred filling her dark, narrowed eyes. Her thin face, encircled by a halo of brittle gray hair, lined with the dust of roads traveled, seemed to grow darker. Her lips curled, exposing uneven, yellowed teeth. Her eyes never leaving Nick, she defiantly drew back her head, then, leaning forward, deliberately spat into the well.

"A curse upon you," she hissed. "And upon your children and even your children's children." Then, gathering her water bags, she turned upon her heel and limped back to her waiting comrades.

Nick remained beside the well until the dilapidated wagon had disappeared beyond the grove of oak trees. He was surprised to find Mattie waiting for him on the veranda steps, her face ashen.

"Oh, Nick, a curse. She put a curse upon our well."

Nick slipped an arm around Mattie's shoulder. "Pay her no mind, Pug. She's just a vagabond, a gypsy. It's just senseless superstition, it means nothing."

*   *   *   *

It was not long after when an already battered South buckled beneath yet another onslaught; typhoid. Stealthily, the highly infectious disease crawled across the land, crept into gardens to taint the food growing there. Slipping into lazy streams, seeping into the soil to contaminate Nature's underground reservoirs, it eventually found its way into the well providing water for the family of Nicholas Brisky IV.

* * * *

Young Nicholas was the first to fall ill, writhing with pain as the infection tore at his insides. Shuddering chills alternated with the fever draining life from his body. Mattie hovered over her oldest son, wrapping him in warm blankets, bathing his burning skin from bedside pans of water, forcing its coolness between his lips to replenish the moisture being pillaged from him. Next it was Susan then Alvie who took to their bed with the dreaded disease. One by one, as her children fell victim, the water supply, carried in buckets from the well, stored in large vessels upon the kitchen counter, became one of Mattie's primary concerns. The cooling liquid was her only ally in the battle against this illness, soothing hot fevered bodies, relieving dry, parched throats.

It was late August, the season when violent summer storms invade the Southland. Exploding grenades of lightening join earth and sky, barrages of raindrops pelt the thirsty Alabama soil. It was on such a night when, Nick having relieved her of her vigil at Susan's bedside, an exhausted Mattie stumbled into the kitchen to recheck the water containers and the crucial level of the precious liquid they held. Obsessed with the constancy of their water supply, she knew she could not rest until she made another trip to the well. Taking no heed of the elements, she struggled up the pathway. Her arms ached, straining at the winch as she cranked the water-filled pail to the top of the well.

Mattie reached for the brimming wooden bucket, closed her hand about its metal handle. A jagged spear of lightening shot across the sky, split open the dark, heavy clouds, freeing the turbulent maelstrom trapped inside. Mattie's hand released its hold, the water bucket crashed back into the depths of the well as a sudden burst of electricity jolted through her body wrenching a terrified scream of pain from her lips.

* * * *

Doctor Willis leaned over Mattie's sleeping form, his hand resting upon her forehead, then straightening, turned to face the man hovering at the end of the four-postered bed. "She's lucky the water bucket absorbed most of the charge. She'll be all right, Nick. Just see that she gets a couple of days bed rest."

Anxiety slowly eased itself from Nick's ashen face. "She will, Doc. I'll make sure of that."

"As for your youngsters, little Nicholas, Susan, Alvie..." The doctor paused. "Well, I guess you can only keep doing what you've been doing and hope for the best." The latch snapped shut as he closed his black bag of cure-alls and turned to leave. "Never mind seeing me to the door, Nick. I'll let myself out." He hesitated, his hand on the doorknob. "Oh, by the way, Nick, there's been some concern about underground reservoirs becoming contaminated. You might want to start boiling your drinking water, just to be on the safe side."

Chapter 16

"It was the gypsy! <u>She</u> killed my babies! The gypsy killed my babies!"

The shrill, reedy voice pierced the stillness of the crowded train station. It fell harshly upon the ears of waiting travelers, momentarily snatching their attention from glossy pages of print or wooly rows of knits and purls. Curious eyes darted toward the frail figure of a woman, her pale face framed by a tangle of unkempt hair poking from beneath the dark shroud covering her head. Then, self-conscious glances turned away as they met the defiant glare of the tall man near her who rose quickly to his feet.

Giving his young son's shoulder a reassuring squeeze, Nick moved swiftly to the woman's side. Lowering his lanky frame onto one knee, bringing his gentle eyes level with her troubled ones, Nick wrapped his work-roughened hands around his wife's cold fingers.

"It's all right, Pug," he soothed. "Everything is going to be all right."

Nick glanced along the row of his children, silently huddled on the hard wooden bench beside their mother. The germ of doubt plaguing him these past weeks flared within him as ten pair of solemn, trusting eyes stared back at him. With a confidence he did not feel, Nick forced a reassuring smile to his lips. He let his gaze slide beyond the children, to where all the possessions they could bring with them stood in a pitiful stack on the station's platform. Another, smaller stack, wicker baskets, packed with enough chicken and cornbread to feed his family during the long journey, waited at the end of the wooden bench.

Nick swallowed against the uneasy lump of fear crouching in the back of his throat. Was he doing the right thing? It was a question he'd asked himself over and over. Was it wrong to move his family from the only home they knew, into a strange, wild territory where their future was so uncertain? He turned his attention back to Mattie, wishing he could snatch away the unattractive, black hood covering her head. She'd worn it since the night of the storm when, drawing water from the well, she'd been struck by a bolt of lightening. She complained thereafter of always being cold. But Nick suspected it was more than coldness she sought to hide beneath that handmade bit of cloth. Not knowing the well was contaminated, she'd continued to urge its tainted waters into the mouths of her children in an effort to wash away the terrible fever accompanying the typhoid sickness. Nick knew she blamed herself for their deaths.

Young William, only fifteen years old, was the first to be taken from them on the fourth day of September. One year old Thomas followed him on the twenty-third day of the same month; Susan, aged nineteen, on the twenty eighth day, thirteen-year-old Alvie on September thirtieth, and finally, his oldest son, Nicholas, succumbed to the merciless epidemic. Nick began to seriously consider his brother William's offer of the land he owned in the Pacific Northwest. Now, standing in this crowded train station, Nick's doubts once again assailed him. Had his decision been the best for his family, or a terrible mistake?

"The gypsy. It was the gypsy."

Salty tears stung Nick's eyelids at the plaintive sound of his wife's voice.

Instinctively, his hand tightened over hers. It had to be the right decision, for Mattie's sake. "Hush, Mattie, he whispered. "It's over now. You must try to forget."

But even as he spoke, Nick knew neither of them could ever forget the five children they were leaving behind, children who were now only names carved into cold slabs of stone. He was just as certain, he would never convince Mattie it was not the gypsy and her terrible curse that killed their children.

* * * *

It had been a long journey; twelve days upon this train carrying them to their destination. Mattie exhausted, the children restless, Nick welcomed a surge of overwhelming relief when the conductor finally announced their arrival in the little town of Cashmere. Nick set about gathering their belongings; pillows, blankets, baskets, when excited squeals erupting from the compartment housing the children, interrupted him. Hurrying to the cubicle, he discovered the youngsters crowded about the window, noses pressed against its pane, as they stared out into the brightness beyond. Glancing over their heads, he too, could not suppress his own gasp of wonder. The ground, the rooftops, everything was covered with a white, powdery substance. It was beautiful, breath-taking.

"Snow!" Nick exclaimed.

He could barely contain his ecstatic children as they crowded past him and into the aisle, each eager to be the first to experience this wonderful phenomena. Fortunately, the Mission Hotel, where they would spend the night, stood directly across from the train station. For, by the time they traversed the short distance, every child had absorbed a good deal of the moisture and was sopping wet.

The following morning, another delight awaited them. A horse-drawn sleigh, driven by their uncle, awaited them outside the hotel, ready to take them on an exciting ride across the snow-covered countryside. Since limited space within the sled accommodated only a few children at a time, it was necessary to make several trips before the impatience of each and every child had been satisfied. Not until then did Nick and William set out for the valley where Nick's family would soon settle.

The heavy sleigh slid easily along the narrow track, the sharp blades of its runners cutting deep slashes into the new fallen snow. Nick feasted his eyes on the pristine beauty surrounding them. Timbered hills rose up on either side of the quiet valley, tall evergreens bowed their branches beneath the weight of wet snow; jackrabbits, quail, pheasant, even deer, all leaving their telltale footprints across the powdery whiteness.

He turned to his brother. "You certainly didn't exaggerate, William. I don't see how you can bear to leave it."

William was silent, his eyes on the roadway ahead. "Yes, it is beautiful, Nick," he agreed. "But it can also be cruel, so very cruel."

* * * *

Nick chose the spot where he would build his home but not at the base of the hill, the scar of the avalanche still painfully visible. He chose, instead, a site directly in the center of the canyon floor, next to the cool waters of a bubbling brook. It was February; snow still covered the ground. It would April before construction could be completed. But at last it arrived, that proud day in April, when, his arm about Mattie's waist, Nick stood upon a grassy knoll, admiring the culmination of his efforts. Although not as grandiose as the mansion they left in Alabama, this simple, two-story frame house was a beginning; a new beginning, for the family of Nicholas Brisky IV.

Chapter 17

▼

A few swift thrusts upon the pump's handle and cold, spring water spurted from the spout, swirling into the wooden trough below. Stripping off his shirt, Nick plunged his hands into the icy liquid, splashing it onto his face, across the back of his neck. Rivulets of the frigid water ran down his arms and chest, carrying with them the sickly green film covering the exposed areas of Nick's body. Grabbing the worn towel from its hook beside the wash stand, he quickly swabbed away the tainted moisture. Aware of how it disturbed Mattie, seeing him covered with the toxic substance, he hoped to remove its unsightly evidence before facing his wife.

"It's a poison, Nick," Mattie fretted. "If it's so lethal to insects, how can you be sure it won't affect you?"

"Don't worry, Pug," he comforted her. "It 's not harmful to humans." But, in truth, he had little confidence in his own words of reassurance.

There was no choice, he told himself. Insects, pests, disease, all were a threat to the vulnerable apples and pears. Early spring spraying was necessary if he was to protect his crops from later infestation. Just as important was pruning weaker, volunteer shoots from fruit-bearing branches before the tiny pink and white blossoms appeared to fill the spring air with their sweet fragrance. Just as later, clusters of the little green orbs replacing the blossoms, needed to be carefully reduced to one in order to provide room for growth of the remaining fruit. Nick had learned each step was necessary if he expected a healthy crop.

Crossing to the porch, Nick plucked the freshly laundered shirt from where Mattie had draped it across the railing. Slipping his arms into the garment's sleeves, Nick let his eyes wander across the land surrounding the big, two-story frame house to where, alongside the packing shed where fruit was sorted and boxed for market, a haughty detachment of smooth-barked cherry trees commandeered the coveted flat land. To the north, beyond the buildings housing the livestock, a field of alfalfa, lazily swaying in the gentle breeze, separated the barnyard from stunted-in-stature but tenacious orchards of apricots and pears. On the slope just south of the house, regimented rows of gnarly-trunk apple trees marched stoically up the gentle rise of the hillside.

A smile crept across Nick's face and a warm surge of pride flowed through him. It had been a challenge, he admitted. With no slaves, this time, to lighten the burden, he, his sons alongside him, had succeeded in building a new empire. The sudden awakening of a suppressed heartache knotted itself in Nick's chest as the painful memory of his oldest son re-surfaced. Nicholas whose birthright this would have been, who should have been here to carry on the name that had been his father's, his grandfather's, now lay cold beneath the soil of Alabama. *Ah well*, Nick pushed the unwelcome thoughts from his mind. *There can be no changing what fate has decreed.*

It had been a good challenge for Mattie, he decided; teaching their daughters to plant and tend the garden, then preserve food to sustain them through the long winter months. She had seemed almost like the 'old Mattie' again. A dark scowl crowded the smile from his face. *If only she'd get rid of that unsightly black hood.*

The screech of a chicken hawk, circling overhead, brought Nick back to the present. The noisy chatter of the poppin-johnny no longer tatooed the air. Its silence assured Nick his sons, John and Guy, had abandoned their chore of cutting fuel for the wood-burning stove and were now, as was he, responding to the summons of the big iron dinner bell to the noon day meal.

"I don't want this food getting cold," Mattie's scolded from beyond the kitchen's screen door. "Are the boys here yet?"

"I don't hear the poppin-johnny." Nick knew his sons, as well as he, were aware of their mother's insistence on promptness. "I expect Guy and John are on their way."

"What about George? Can you see if he's started down the hill yet?"

Quickly securing the remaining buttons of his shirt, Nick focused his attention upon the area above the apple trees. He let his eyes slowly traced the journey of the weathered wood flume crawling across the hillside, carrying its supply of metered water from the sluice box to the thirsty orchards. His search was rewarded when he caught sight of George, shovel in hand, urging a final trickle of water into the hand-dug irrigation ditches before responding to the mid-day meal call.

Yet the germ of uncertainty, once planted in Nick's mind, took root and sprouted. His thoughts returned to his earlier concern. Which of his sons shared his dreams, he wondered? Who would be the one to step into his shoes? While doubt and indecision filled his mind, it was the tantalizing smell of freshly baked bread finally luring him up the porch steps and into the kitchen.

* * * *

Having passed Mattie's poorly concealed scrutiny for any lingering traces of the hated green toxin Nick turned his attention to his sons seated across from him at the oilcloth-covered kitchen table. The earlier good-natured chatter gave way to the clatter of silverware as the hungry men focused upon the steaming bowls of hearty beef stew and fragrant slabs of homemade bread set before them. Nick studied the sun-darkened faces gathered about his table and once again his question re-surfaced. Which of these three strapping young men, he wondered, shared his dream? All had helped in the building of his empire, yet Nick was fairly certain not all were cut out to be farmers. He doubted if his one absent son, Jesse, off fighting the Germans, would ever be content with this way of life. But what about the others, he pondered.

"Quit hoggin' the bread, John."

Nick glanced toward him as John, unsmilingly, relinquished the now depleted-by-half platter of sliced bread to his brother. Would it be John, Nick asked himself? The oldest of his sons now, John somehow seemed uncomfortable with his senior status, his attitude defensive, often overbearing; the performance of his duties less than enthusiastic.

"Hey, Inez" Guy directed his question to where his sister stood at the counter of the buffet-like "kitchen queen," skimming the heavy cream from pans filled with the morning's milking. Nick's daughters, while sharing the family supper, did not join the men for the mid-day meal. "We got any of those cucumber pickles left?" Guy queried

As Inez crossed to the ice box to fill Guy's request, Nick shifted his attention toward his youngest son. What of Guy, he mused? Sandy haired, easy going, the opposite of his older brother, he took nothing in life seriously. His boyish good looks and easy humor made him a favorite with the local ladies. A frown plucked at Nick's forehead. Reports had drifted back to him of Guy's Saturday night escapades, his fondness for the ladies, and the whiskey.

That left George. Nick turned his eyes toward the second oldest of his sons. A handsome young man, Nick admitted, with his mother's Irish features, her auburn tinged hair. Nick let his thoughts drift back over the years to when they first arrived in Cashmere, when the children first played in the snow. George was only eleven then. Even at that early age, George's was a quiet display of responsibility. It had not gone unnoticed when he eventually assumed the "older brother" role toward his sisters appointing himself chaperone in later years when they attended dances or local boy/girl functions. Studying the genial face across the table, Nick considered his son's current social life. While enjoying his popularity with the single young women, George showed, to their consternation, no inclination to choose a wife. His energies seemed centered upon the ranch and tending to its fragile crops.

Chairs scraped against wooden floorboards as they were moved back from the table. Sated appetites spawned friendly smiles and good-natured ribaldry as the young farmers returned to their chores. Watching his sons file from the kitchen, a smile softened Nick's own suntanned features. Mentally, he made note to have a talk with George soon, very soon.

Chapter 18

Nick never regretted his decision to entrust the ranch's operation to his middle son. It was Nick's daughters who first, one by one, married and left the homestead, Aletha, Nan and Carrie, then Mattie, Inez and Ruth. Nick would sometimes wonder why none married a rancher. Eventually, John took a wife and moved into town, soon followed by Guy and his new spouse. Nick knew a keener disappointment when neither pursued a farming career. Nick had been right about his soldier son Jesse who returned from the war but not to the ranch. He and his bride moved across the mountains to the greener shores of Puget Sound. Only George remained, working at Nick's side, enlarging the orchards, harvesting the crops, making Nick's dream his own.

The late summer crop of 1925 was a bountiful one. 'Apple knockers' were filling the bins with the ripening, bright red fruit. Long pole props, used to support heavy branches laden with fruit, now stood in tepeed clusters at the edge of the orchard.

"It's about time to get the packing shed into operation," His son beside him, Nick strode through the orchard, carefully inspecting crates overflowing with the day's harvest. "The box assemblers should be starting production and we need to line up a crew of sorters and packers."

"Got it covered, Dad." Snatching a delicious apple from the bin, George polished it against his blue denim shirt before crunching into its crispness, letting the opulent juices dribble down his chin. "There's a batch of applicants showing up tomorrow morning at eight. I'll have them at the conveyer belt and working by nine."

*   *   *   *

George moved down the row of applicants lined up before him, nodding toward each familiar face of seasonal workers who showed up every fall, seeking work in the Brisky packing shed. He hesitated in front of a young woman he'd not seen before. Petite, pretty, he noticed, he'd guess her to be no more than eighteen years of age.

"I don't think I've met you. You new in town?"

"I'm spending the summer with relatives," she explained shyly, her voice barely above a whisper.

A refreshing change, George decided, from the rather plain, local females who openly smiled and flirted with him, the town's thirty-two-year-old most eligible bachelor.

"You ever sorted apples before Miss … Miss …?"

"Brooks. Evelyn Brooks," she blushed. "No, but if someone will show me how, I can learn."

As willing as the new young sorter was to learn, Nick noticed George was equally as willing to teach her, displaying patience he seldom afforded the other hired hands. As his son began spending more and more time at the young woman's station, Nick watched the obvious flirtation blossom. It came as no surprise to him when, at the end of harvest season, George proposed marriage to Evelyn, and she accepted.

It was November when couple drove to the courthouse in Wenatchee to be married. Stars in her eyes, Evelyn smiled into the photographer's camera before they headed back to the ranch. Any dreams she may have had of a romantic honeymoon dissolved the moment they entered the house. A horse was 'down' in the barnyard, Nick informed them; the plow horse they bought only yesterday. Her heart heavy with disappointment, Evelyn watched her new husband slip quickly into a pair of coveralls and hurry out the door with his father. It wasn't until then she became aware of Pug, standing at her elbow, a large, bulging laundry bag in her hand. She extended it to Evelyn.

"I suspect now that you're George's wife, you'll be wanting to do his washing."

Her salty tears mixed with soapy suds as Evelyn spent the first day of her honeymoon, bent over a tin washtub, scrubbing green, toxic residue from a pair of George's overalls.

*   *   *   *

Harvest season was over; apples, cherries, pears and apricots picked, packed and sold at market. Alfalfa had been mowed, shocked then pitched into the barn's hayloft from where it would be doled to the animals during the long winter months. Pigs had been butchered; salt cured ham hocks hung in the corncrib alongside drying ears of corn. Vegetables from the garden had been canned and stored in the earthen cellar beneath the house. Berries were turned into jam; sauerkraut set to curing. Lower grade 'cull' apples were forced through the hand-turned press, their juices left to ferment into cider. Chores still ate up most of the day but there was time now for George to begin construction on a little two-bedroom house less than a mile away from the big house. By spring, Evelyn and George would be able to move into a home of their own.

Meanwhile, both John and Guy remained in town. John had found gainful employment but Guy had not fared so well. His family of seven had outgrown their two-bedroom home but, unable to hold a steady job, Guy could not afford to move them into larger living quarters. Nick knew it was because Guy, still winsome, boyish, irresponsible, had taken whisky as his mistress. While Nick was aware George and Evelyn supplied Guy's family with food from their own larder, he said nothing. He remained silent even when he learned Guy's wife was suggesting an institutional "cure" for her husband.

"I guess it's a frontal lobotomy or the bottle in front of me," Guy had quipped

Nick harbored no sympathy for his youngest son, had no tolerance for his weakness for the spirits. His concern, instead, was for his own wife, Pug. She seemed to have lost her endurance for the cold winters, took longer recovering from more frequent colds and seasonal maladies. He watched her this morning as she moved slowly about the kitchen performing the habitual chores of breakfast preparation, the hateful, now ever-present black shroud pulled snugly about her ears.

"Are you feeling okay, Pug?"

"I'm fine, Nick, just a little tired. I think it might be a touch of the flu."

Worry furrowed Nick's brow. "Maybe you should go see Dr. Schumaker," he suggested. "I'll drive you in this morning."

"No, no, I'll be fine, Nick. Just as soon as I get warmed up, I'll be fine."

But Nick remained unconvinced. His concern continued to grow when, during the following weeks, her strength did not return. In January of 1929 Nick's emotional world came crashing down around him. Unable to recover from this most recent bout with the flu, Pug quietly surrendered to death.

* * * *

Nick was delighted when George, Evelyn and their two small daughters decided to move back into the big house. It didn't seem so empty with small, happy children underfoot once again. It pleased him, too, when John returned to the homestead, moving his family into the recently vacated little house, now nearly bursting at its seams. For John's family, too, had grown larger in number, larger than he could comfortably afford. Nick lifted an eyebrow when he overheard George, perhaps less than discreetly, suggest that perhaps his brother should consider balancing the size of his family with his income.

As usual, a serious-minded John took refuge in his Bible quotations. "The Lord," John retorted, "has said 'Go forth and replenish the earth.'"

Nick hid an irrepressible chuckle behind a callused hand "Yes, John," had been George's caustic reply. "But he didn't mean all by yourself."

However, it was his daughter-in-law Evelyn who troubled Nick's peace of mind of late. He'd paid little attention to her while Pug was alive; the women kept pretty much to themselves. But now, sharing the same roof, he recalled his wife's comments about George's little English bride and her determination to raise her daughters as "proper young ladies". Evelyn was a pretty little thing, Nick admitted, but so ... petite. It couldn't be easy for her adjusting to their ways. He admired her stubborn tenacity. Making up for her lack of strength, it enabled her to take on chores far too heavy for her tiny frame. Farming was a hard life but Nick never heard his daughter-in-law complain. He never heard her laugh, either, or saw her smile. He saw only a wistful sadness in her eyes. As sure as he was Evelyn loved her husband, Nick was just as sure she was a very unhappy young woman.

While he didn't hold with sticking his nose into other people's business, he thought maybe he should have a talk with his daughter-in-law. But before he could act on his decision, other problems arose to demand his time. Even with John's help, the year's crop proved to be not a good one. His many years at farming had taught Nick to accept the instability of apple ranching.

"We'll be fine; just have to tighten our belts for the winter," he assured his sons. "Next year's crop will be better." It was October 1929. Nick's financial world was about to crash, along with the New York stock market.

*   *   *   *

The following year's apple crop was not good. Nick and his family faced financial jeopardy. They would not go hungry; food for their families would come from the farm.

But there was no money to fund next year's crop. Nick refused to part with the ranch's livestock, the horses; the cows. But there were John's pigs. The sows had recently given birth to their litters. Nearly one hundred squealing piglets were squirming and crawling over one another in the pig barn.

"We've butchered enough pork to feed ourselves," Nick announced to his sons. "George, you take the shoats to Ed Simpson. He's always paid five dollars apiece for them. They oughta bring us enough cash to buy the spray dope we'll need."

But Ed Simpson did not pay five dollars apiece for the shoats. Money was tight for him, too. "One dollar," he apologized to George. "One dollar apiece is all I can give you."

The banker at Cashmere Valley Bank had always been not only their friend but also their financial backer. The depression tied his hands. He could no longer gamble on the instability of a bleeding economy. "I can take a mortgage on your next year's apple crop," he offered Nick. "It's the best I can do."

Helpless, Nick could only watch as his empire crumbled about him. In June of 1933, discouraged, heart broken, he slipped away to join his "Pug" in death.

The following year, George's wife presented him with a son, a son they called Nicholas.

NICHOLAS V
1933–

Chapter 19

▼

"I can't believe you'd do such a thing!"

Nicholas cringed at the sound of his father's voice, distorted by rage. Hoping to make himself less visible, he pressed his frail body deeper into the protective corner of the couch. The rough horsehair fabric bit through the thin flannel of his pajamas, gnawing at the tenderness of his young skin. Across the room, poised for battle, sat the two most important people in his life.

Nicholas had never seen his parents so angry, bruising the air with the harshness of their accusations; hurtling vicious words at one another, like sharpened darts, meant to pierce an opponent's ego. Theirs were strange, unfamiliar words; words five-year-old Nicholas was too young to understand; "depression, mortgage, self-respect."

"Have you no pride?" Anger darkened the face Nicholas' father turned toward his wife.

Nicholas scrunched further into the depths of the divan, seeking obscurity in its abrasive embrace. Sent to his bed half an hour earlier, he'd listened to the verbal conflict being waged in the adjoining room. Finally, too frightened to sleep, he crept quietly back into the living room, finding security, albeit unsettling, in the physical presence of his parents.

It was winter outside; snow still clung to the frozen ground. Inside, a fire burned in the big stone fireplace, its flames munching upon a feast of dry logs. Crackling contentedly, it seemed oblivious to the chill of hostility filling the room. Nicholas shivered. From what he could gather, his mother and father were fighting over "hard times," "pride" … and his new shoes.

Nicholas' gaze flew to the pair of shoes now resting atop the low table in front of the fireplace. Once again, he was filled with the same warm glow he'd felt when he'd first laid eyes upon them. A grand pair of shoes, they were, the grandest shoes he'd seen in all his young life.

They'd gone to the J C Penny store this afternoon, he and his mother, to buy him a new pair of shoes, another pair of those high top, 'sensible' cloth tennis shoes he so hated. The clerk had gone to check on sizes when, slouched sullenly in his chair, Nicholas glanced up and there, perched proudly upon the top shelf, their shiny black leather tops winking in the overhead lights, were a pair of shoes, the likes of which he'd not known existed. A yearning welled up within him, a yearning so overwhelming, he could taste it on the back of his tongue. Totally engrossed, he failed to notice the man crossing from the far side of the store to speak softly to the clerk. Not until the smooth leather of those beautiful shoes was sliding over his feet, hugging his toes, clinging to his heels, did he glance up, a giddy smile upon his face.

He recognized him then, his benefactor, smiling across at Nicholas' mother. It was their neighbor, the one who lived down the road, the one who came so often to visit his father. Nicholas' father was usually working in the orchards, but the man would stay and drink coffee with Nicholas' mother and make her smile and laugh. Nicholas didn't like the man, but instead of offering his usual scowl, Nicholas returned his attention to those grand shoes, feasting his eyes on their shiny blackness, filling his nostrils with their fragrance of new leather. Today they had made him very, very happy. But tonight, they were making his father very, very angry.

"You'd begrudge your son a decent pair of shoes just because of your stupid pride?" His mother's voice was shrill, accusing.

"I can provide for my own children!" His defensive retort brought Nicholas' father to his feet. "I don't need charity!"

In the next instant, a gasp of horror escaped Nicholas' lips as, in one swift motion, his father snatched the shoes from the tabletop and flung them into the fireplace where excited flames leaped to greet them.

Somewhere a door slammed, a woman sobbed, but Nicholas' only awareness was of his wonderful, grand shoes being devoured by greedy, yellow tongues of fire. Shiny black leather curled amidst the heat, the stench of burning rubber filled the air until, finally, those wonderful, grand shoes were no more than charred, smoldering lumps of gray.

* * * *

The aroma of frying bacon slipped beneath his bedroom door, nudging Nicholas to wakefulness. Poorly muted sounds of breakfast preparation clattered from the direction of the kitchen. Shoving aside the cotton quilt, Nicholas slid from his bed, wriggling into the jean pants and flannel shirt he'd worn the day before. Once his feet were inside his wool socks, he bent to retrieve his shoes. A sharp pang of remembering filled his chest. The salty moisture of threatening tears stung his eyelids.

Defiantly kicking aside the old high top tennis shoes standing obediently at the bedside, he stomped across the room in his stocking feet. He was just reaching for its round glass knob when the bedroom door opened. Nicholas found himself looking up into the tear-reddened eyes of the man who, last night, had sacrificed a grand pair of shoes to appease a fit of anger. Nicholas stepped back, catering, for a moment, to his own anger. In the next moment, his father was kneeling before him, gathering his son into his arms.

"You be a good boy, Nicholas." His father's voice was thick with unshed tears. "I'm counting on you to look after your mother and the girls." He hesitated, an unfamiliar sound strangling his words and Nicholas realized his father was crying. "You'll have to be the man of the family, now," he choked and then, he was gone.

Nicholas stood staring at the empty doorway. *What did his father mean?* His only answer was the sharp click of the metal latch as the front door closed.

* * * *

The days that followed were difficult, confusing days for Nicholas. Everything was different and he didn't know why. There was a silence shrouding the house, a silence that had never been there before. He could usually tease one of his sisters into "catch-me-if-you-can" chase but now, they both ignored him. Mealtimes were the worst, with his father's empty chair staring at them from the head of the table. One day he wandered into the kitchen to find his mother, standing at the kitchen sink, crying. People he'd never seen before were prowling through the house, even invading the upstairs bedrooms where strangers were never allowed. More than once he heard whispered conversations that included the word "divorce." It was all very confusing for Nicholas.

It was Saturday morning. The younger of Nicholas' two sisters, the one he could antagonize the easiest, moved lethargically about the sunroom, swiping haphazardly at the piano's surface with the dust cloth clutched in her hand. Crawling up on the piano bench, he tucked his feet beneath him and waited for his sister to acknowledge his transgression upon this forbidden perch. For awhile, she continued to ignore him and then, as he knew she would finally do, she whirled to face him.

"What do you want?" she demanded, dark eyes snapping with anger.

Nicholas was silent for a moment, then, sighed deeply. "I want to know, what is a divorce?"

His sister glared at him, not speaking. "Stupid!" She all but spat the words at her little brother. "Don't you know anything? Divorce means Mama and Daddy aren't going to be married anymore. It means we can't live in this house anymore, somebody else is going to live here. It means we have to move into town with Mama and that Daddy won't ..." Nicholas saw tears filling his sister's eyes. "Oh, you are so stupid. You don't know anything!"

Nicholas stared after his sister's departing figure, then at the dust cloth she'd flung to the floor. He slid his feet from beneath him, studied the ugly high top tennis shoes now dangling in front of him. *Was it possible,*

Nicholas wondered. *Could his entire life have changed all because of a pair of shoes?*

Chapter 20

Nicholas snapped open the lid covering his sister's portable record player. Reaching beneath her bed, he pulled out the box where he knew she stored her twelve-inch phonograph records. Idly, he sorted through the collection; Glen Miller, Frank Sinatra, the Ink Spots, Spike Jones. He hesitated, his hand resting upon his sister's favorite, Rhapsody in Blue. No, better not. If he so much as put a scratch on it, she'd kill him for sure. He flicked on to the next platter, one he hadn't seen before, Porgy and Bess. Slipping the brittle black circle from its cardboard jacket, he dropped it onto the spindle and lowered the machine's arm onto the spinning disk.

Crawling up onto the patchwork bedspread, he elbowed a stoic brown teddy bear from its perch of prominence. Punching the pillow into a soft ball behind him, he leaned back against the headboard. A self-satisfied smile scampered across his young face. Boy, his sister would have a fit if she knew he was messing with her records. To say nothing of how mad his mom would be if she knew he was skipping school.

"Summer time, and the living is easy," sang a woman with a too-high voice.

Playing hooky was pretty "easy," too, Nicholas smirked. All he had to do was head out after breakfast like he was going to school. Once he was sure his mom had left for work and his sister was on her way to school, he doubled back and had the apartment to himself for the whole day. He didn't have to worry about the school checking with his mom because she was at work. It was a perfect plan but, of course, he didn't do it very often. That would be too risky.

"I got plenty of nothin'." It was a man singing now.

His words were kind of hard to understand but Nicholas knew just how the singer felt. It was exactly the way he felt about school, 'plenty of nothin'. Nicholas snatched up the dethroned teddy bear and glared into its reproachful agate-colored eyes. "I hate this school," he hissed. "I hate this town. I hate this apartment." He'd hated all those other schools, too, he remembered. All those other towns and the other places they'd lived. But most of all, he hated that first school, the one he'd gone to after they left the ranch. Memories rekindled his angry defiance and he drove his doubled-up fist into teddy's soft little tummy. He'd been lonesome, his first time away from home, away from his mother. But he had also been frightened, frightened by the bigger boys who, maybe because he was small for his age, took delight in heckling him out in the schoolyard.

Avoiding the playground at recess wasn't a problem but during lunchtime, no one was allowed to stay in the classroom. A crafty smile eased the anger tightening Nicholas' face. Then was when he'd had learned how to outsmart his tormentors. Dawdling at his desk, he made sure he was the last to leave the room. Then, at just the right moment, he'd duck beneath the teacher's desk where he could eat his lunch, undetected and undisturbed.

The music rising from the phonograph had grown louder, drums thumping and horns blaring. Did his sister really like this kind of music, Nicholas wondered? He liked her recording of "Twilight Time" a lot better except it made him feel sad, really lonesome deep inside. But he felt that way most of the time anymore. It would be nice if he could have a dog to keep him company. His father said he could have a dog but then that would only be on the weekends he spent with his father. Nicholas wanted a dog he could have with him all the time, even when he stayed with his mother. But she said they couldn't have a pet in the apartment.

"I bet if I threatened to go live with Dad, she'd let me have one anyway," he boasted to his dethroned captive.

Sometimes Nicholas daydreamed about what it would be like living with his father, out in the country. But then he'd remember the morning when he was only five, his father holding him and telling him he would have to be the man of the family. After the divorce, he'd said, Nicholas' mother and sisters would need someone to look after them. Nicholas sighed. He could only do that if he stayed in this apartment, in this city where he had to attend this crummy school. The little stuffed animal once became again the object of its captor's abuse.

"Nicholas!"

The fuzzy brown teddy slipped from its tormenter's fingers and tumbled to the floor as startled, Nicholas looked up. His mother stood in the bedroom doorway, her face dark with anger.

"What are you doing home? Why aren't you in school?"

* * * *

Nicholas was eleven years old when, just as his father had done six years earlier, his mother knelt before him, gathering her son in her arms.

"We must be brave, Nicholas," she insisted though the tears streaming down her face belied her own inadequate strength. "You are growing into a young man, now. So your father and I have decided it best you live with him." Her eyes pleaded for his understanding. "Please, Nicholas. Remember, I'll always love you."

Chapter 21

For the next six years, Nicholas would work alongside his father in the little grocery store/café his father built when he first moved to Seattle. Nicholas liked it because, even though it was at the junction of three busy highways, it was out in the country and he could have his dog. But he missed his mother. She had moved to Alaska and then on to California so he never saw her. Sometimes he missed his two sisters; one had married; the other lived in an apartment in the city. He seldom saw either of them. So, mostly, it was just he and his dad and his dog. He was enrolled in school in the neighboring town of Bellevue, where he faithfully attended classes every day. He suspected his father would have little tolerance with truancy. After-school hours were spent helping his father in the store. It became a daily routine.

He soon realized his father was totally dedicated to the operation of his business, had no interest in anything outside the market. It wasn't long before Nicholas became bored with the monotony of his life.

"You're getting a hands on business education," his father would remind him. "A lesson in responsibility."

But Nicholas was a young boy, not ready for the burden of responsibility. The same restlessness plaguing his mother also flowed in his veins. Instead of gratitude for this gift of a business education, he felt only resentment.

It was 1951 when Nicholas graduated from high school. He knew he would now be expected to spend even more hours in the store; to make it his life. He tried to emulate his father's stability, his dedication to running a grocery business. But by the end of the summer, Nicholas felt smothered beneath the burden. After many sleepless nights, he decided to be honest with his father.

*   *   *   *

It was Sunday morning. Sundays were always slow, people sleeping in or attending church. Nicholas and his father tarried over their morning coffee. The young man stared into the black liquid filling his cup.

"You know, Dad," he began. "I'm not sure this is what I want to do with my life."

The old man stirred another spoonful of sugar into his own coffee. "Give it time, Son," he soothed. "It's a good honest way to make a living. Just give yourself time. You'll do fine."

"But, Dad …"

"I was thinking this might be a good time to go over the produce figures," his father suggested. "We lost a lot on tomatoes last week. Maybe we should cut back on our order." He spread the sales sheet out upon the counter.

Nicholas knew their conversation was over.

Only two days had passed when his father called him into the back office. "I've been thinking, Son," he announced. "An ice cream parlor might be a good addition to our business. We can add onto the west side of the building, there's room there." A self-satisfied smile creased the older man's face. "I'm putting you in charge," he added proudly. "It'll be yours to run anyway you see fit."

A heavy mantle of despair and guilt settled itself upon Nicholas' shoulders. It was obvious his father was trying to make the market more appealing to him, to discourage any thoughts he might have of leaving. So Nicholas tried, he tried so very hard, but the demons of restlessness would not be stilled.

*   *   *   *

It was past nine o'clock. The doors to the market were closed and secured. Sounds of clattering dishes and clinking silverware drifting from next door indicated the café was also shutting down for the night. Nicholas and his father stood at the cash register, tallying the day's receipts. Nicholas shifted the stack of Sunday newspapers resting on the counter, the front headlines heralding the unrest in Korea.

"Looks like we're really getting involved in Korea," he began uneasily.

His father grunted his acknowledgement.

Nicholas filled his lungs with air, hoping to fortify the decision he'd made earlier. "Dad." Reluctant words cowered in his throat, then rushed recklessly past his dry lips.

"Dad, I've decided to join the Navy."

The old man continued to regiment the dog-eared currency between his fingers, only the slight lift of one eyebrow suggesting he'd heard his son. "Well," he finally sighed. "Maybe you just need a break; get away from the store for awhile." His eyes met Nicholas', a sad smile creasing his ruddy features. "Go join your navy, Son. We'll still be here when you're ready to come home."

*   *   *   *

Nicholas had not yet completed his tour of duty when he received the telegram from his sister. "Dad in hospital. Seriously ill. Come home." Although immediate steps were taken to expedite Nick's return, before he arrived home his father had lapsed into a coma from which he never revived.

His father's death not only qualified Nicholas for a "hardship discharge" it forced him into a decision he was reluctant to make. He knew he was expected to take over the business; to step into his father's shoes. But an insatiable wanderlust had not been appeased. After only a few short, restless months, Nicholas left the disposition of their father's business in the hands of his sisters and set out in search of a life of his own.

Chapter 22

▼

Reno, that mecca of excitement and opportunity, became Nicholas' first stop where he landed a job as night clerk at a little motel on the edge of town. Modest but glitzy, it provided an introduction to the exuberant bubble that was Reno. Any earlier misgivings regarding his decision to strike out on his own evaporated as he willingly allowed himself to be drawn into the intoxicating epitome of excessiveness.

It happened during his second month as desk clerk. At one o'clock on a Friday morning, things were usually pretty quiet at the motel. Guests who hadn't gone to bed were at the gaming tables in downtown casinos. His back to the counter as he carefully counted the daily receipts, Nicholas turned at a sound behind him. He barely had time to distinguish a shabby, bearded figure before the wild-eyed bit of humanity was lunging across the desk, a knife glistening in his upraised hand.

Nicholas recoiled but not soon enough. He felt the sharp pain as the man's weapon slashed across his shoulder. He staggered back against the wall, heard room keys jostled from their pigeonholes, clattering to the floor. The would-be-thief, eyes glittering, struggled to his feet. Nicholas realized the man planned to attack again.

Clutching his injured arm, Nicholas twisted from behind the counter. He could feel the sticky warmth of blood soaking his torn shirt. His only concern was to put distance between himself and his obviously drug-crazed assailant. He'd seen enough of those these past weeks to know how unpredictable they could be. He ducked through the entrance leading to the sleeping area, ran down the hallway between the numbered doors. He could hear the footsteps behind him, thudding heavily on the worn carpeting. Frantic, he thought to seek refuge in one of the rooms but knew he would only be cornered there.

He was at the end of the hall, flanked now on one side by the ice machine, on the other, the glass doors leading to the pool area. He stepped through the opened doors, making no effort to slide them shut behind him. His eyes darted left, then right, seeking a shelter of safety. A cleaning cart, left by a careless maid, stood between two potted palms. Nicholas crowded quickly behind it and sank to his knees. Crouching in the tiny space, his breath held captive in his aching lungs, Nicholas listened to the stumbling footsteps, the heavy breathing of his stalker, and silently thanked God for the darkness that was his only ally.

It seemed an eternity before the threatening shuffle was heard no more, the cursing no longer polluted the night air. Still, the blood slowly saturating his shirt, Nicholas remained huddled in his space of safety until the Nevada sun finally rose to chase away the shadows of night.

* * * *

"That's a pretty deep cut." The doctor probed the wound in Nicholas' shoulder, then shook his head. "There is a strong possibility you may never regain complete use of your arm."

It took weeks of therapy to prove the doctor wrong. Once he was totally recovered, Nicholas shook the dust of "Sin City" from his sandals and headed for Los Angeles.

* * * *

Nicholas never regretted his decision to move to the "City of Angels." In fact, he decided he might just have finally found his niche in life. While Los Angeles certainly didn't have the frantic pace of life he'd found in Reno, it had a certain ambience, a definite charm of its own. The weather was ideal, opportunities were there for those looking and its people had a lively lust for life that appealed to Nicholas. Experience he'd acquired from working in his father's café landed him a management position at 'The Doghouse Deli'. Away from the deli, he connected with another entrepreneur and together they ran a sideline business marketing rare antiques and a high quality line of collectibles.

Just when he thought life could get no better, he received a letter from his sister. "I thought you might be interested in knowing Mother has moved back to California," she wrote "She is living in a little town called Venice. It's on the outskirts of Los Angeles. Maybe you know where it is. I am enclosing the address."

Nicholas struggled with the maelstrom of emotions churning inside him as he read and reread those few lines, absorbing the portent of their message. He was being given an opportunity to reunite with the mother he'd not seen in years. Except for an all too short visit at the time of his father's funeral, their nomadic lives had, until now, precluded communication between mother and son. He wasted no time. The address tucked in the pocket of his jacket Nicholas set out for the beach communities dotting the coast east of Los Angeles.

*   *   *   *

The bus doors whooshed shut behind him as Nicholas stepped into the warm sunshine bathing the streets of Santa Monica. Following directions he'd received from the bus driver, he soon found himself on the beachfront boardwalk that would take him to the little town of Venice. He hurried along the picturesque walkway, aware of the expanse of white sand bordering the walk, but his attention turned toward its opposite side where weathered, early 1930 circa houses lined narrow streets. His eyes probed anxiously among black and white street signs in search of one matching the address scrawled on the paper in his pocket. He paused before one aging signpost, its flaking green paint attesting to years of neglect, and squinted up at the bent, almost illegible square of metal attached to its top. "Breeze Avenue." He pulled the scrap of paper from his pocket. Yes, this was it.

Climbing the bank of crumbling concrete steps, he prowled along the uneven surface of the cracked sidewalk, peering at barely discernable house numbers. It wasn't until he stood before the shingle-sided two-story beach house at 26 Breeze Avenue, its corroded brass house numbers so faded as to be almost unidentifiable, that Nicholas began to have second thoughts about his visit. It was entirely possible his mother would not be at home. Perhaps he should have written a note first, telling her he was coming, preparing her for his arrival. It was too late for that now. Taking a deep breath, he approached the arched doorway and pressed the rusting doorbell.

A stout older woman opened the door. An apron tied about her middle, a shawl draped about her shoulders, eyes clouded with suspicion, she scowled at Nicholas.

"Vhat?" she demanded.

Somewhat taken aback by this terse introduction to what he would later discover to be a predominately Jewish community, Nicholas hastened to explain his presence.

"I'm … I'm sorry to bother you," he stammered. "I'm looking for my mother. I was told I might find her at this address. Evelyn …" he hesitated, suddenly aware he didn't know the surname his mother was now using.

A gasp escaped from the woman's lips and the scowl disappeared from her face. "A son, yet." She clasped her hands to her breast. "Oy vey. Liddle Evelina's son." Her eyes grew bright with tears. "Your mama, such a dollink. For her, I'm doink anythink."

"Does she live here?" Nicholas interrupted. "Is she here now?"

"Yes, yes, she is livink here," the old woman cried. "But she is gone now, gone for somethink to eat." She grabbed Nicholas by the shoulders, turning him away from the doorway. "Oy vey. You must hurry to find her," she insisted as she pushed him toward the sidewalk. "Liddle Evelina must be knowink her son is comink home."

Hurrying along the boardwalk, Nicholas had gone but a few blocks before he was standing on the streets of the little town named and fashioned in the likeness of that other little town in Italy. Glancing down the quaint "Old World" streets with their arched facades, he immediately understood why she chose this neighborhood. It perfectly suited the treasured "Little English Lady" memories he had of his mother.

Quickly, he scanned the length of the main street anxious now as to what he would say to her once her found her, the mother he'd not seen for so many years? And what, in fact, would she have to say to him? Then he saw her. Seated alone at a table in front of a sidewalk café, a petite older woman, a saucy, flowered hat perched atop her now graying hair, she wore a flattering suit of black. A pair of black spike-heeled sandals enclosed her tiny feet. Years of denied love welled up inside Nicholas, filled his eyes with tears. Quickly covering the distance between them, he paused beside the table.

"Would you mind if I joined you?" he asked quietly.

The woman glanced up, an obvious polite refusal on her lips. In the next moment, she was clutching her son to her, her tears staining the front of his shirt while Nicholas' own tears watered the artificial flowers that adorned her saucy hat.

* * * *

The years that followed were good years for Nicholas. He had his mother back in his life, and while they continued to live in their own separate worlds, she in Venice, he in Los Angeles, their visits with one another were frequent. His antiques and collectibles business was prospering, his job at the deli secure. For the first time in his life he felt happy, fulfilled.

It was Saturday morning. With the California sun already warming the air, it promised to be another scorcher. Nicholas flicked on the air conditioning, adjusting the temperature to a comfortable sixty-five. Knowing his afternoon shift at the deli would be a warm one, he studied the selection of cotton shirts in his closet. The insistent jingle of the telephone interrupted his inspection. Maybe it was yesterday's client inquiring about the Tiffany lamp he speculated as he lifted the phone from its cradle.

"Hello? Yes, yes, this is Nicholas Brisky." A frown dug its way across Nick's forehead. "Who? Doctor Andrews? Saint Joseph Hospital? I don't understand." The color drained from Nicholas' face. "My mother? A stroke? I'll be right there, Doctor."

* * * *

In time, Nicholas' mother recovered from her stroke, her ability to walk restored. But the doctors shared their doubts she would ever regain her power of speech. Nick wasted no time in the remodel of his home. By the time she was able to leave the hospital, he had completed the downstairs private apartment for his mother. He was determined she would never be alone again. He enlisted the services of Raymond, a young male nurse, as full time caregiver to be with his mother when he could not. A conscientious, caring young man, Raymond soon grew to love Nicholas' mother as his own.

It was cancer that finally took her from him; her death that once again brought him back to the state of Washington. Nicholas joined with his sisters in arranging for her burial in the family plot next to their father. Their parents would be together again, in death, as they had not been in life.

Restlessness had once again set in for Nicholas. He decided to remain in Washington. He opened a business in a commercial mall where, seven days a week, twelve hours a day, he offered a jaded public a unique selection of collectibles and antiques.

* * * *

It had been a particularly trying day. Turning the key in the lock securing the iron grating in front of his shop, Nicholas glanced toward the neighboring retailer who had just secured her own security gate.

"Another twelve hour day, another dollar ninety eight," he quipped.

"I don't know how you do it," the young lady sighed. "Doing this seven days a week would absolutely kill me."

Nicholas' thoughts darted back to the little grocery store on the outskirts of Bellevue and the man who had given him a "hands on" business education. It suddenly occurred to him the total commitment to business he'd once rebelled against he was now emulating.

A fleeting smile momentarily erased the weariness aging Nicholas' face. "It looks like you taught me well, Dad," he whispered softly.

Nicholas did not marry. His business ventures became his wife, his children. It would be his sister who would insure the perpetuity of the "nom de Nicholas" with the birth of her second son.

NICHOLAS VI
1951–

Chapter 23

"Just what do you think you are doing, young man?"

Eight-year-old Nicholas glanced up from the rows of colorful plants he'd so carefully arranged atop the large, overturned cardboard carton. "Oh, hi, Mom." He grinned disarmingly into the angry face of the woman glaring at him from across the makeshift table. "I'm selling posies."

"I can see that," was his mother's sharp retort. "And they're primroses, not posies. I'd like an explanation as to how you acquired these primroses you are selling," she demanded.

A sheepish smile crept across Nicky's face. "I didn't dig up all of them, Mom, just those along the fence. There're still lots of them left in your front flowerbed."

"How could you do this, Nicky? Whatever were you thinking?"

"I'm sorry, Mom. Dad said if I wanted money to spend at the Puyallup Fair, I'd have to earn it myself. I didn't think you'd mind."

Smaller in size than the earlier generations of men who had dipped into the Brisky "gene pool", what Nick lacked in stature, he made up for in determination. The second born son, destined to follow in the shadow an older brother, his star eclipsed by the birth of a younger sister, Nick met the challenge of middle-child invisibility. Armed with a heritage of initiative and creativity, it was a very visible Nicholas who strode through his childhood years.

Nicholas was twenty when he enrolled in the commercial art course at Clover Park Community College. There he met Carolyn. She was nineteen. She was beautiful. She became the love of his life. They were inseparable.

* * * *

It was the end of July, a beautiful summer's day. With no classes to attend and Nick not scheduled for his chef's job until the evening shift, they had the whole day to themselves.

"What do you want to do today, Carolyn?" Nick balanced the telephone between his ear and his shoulder, buttering the piece of toast just ejected from the shiny chrome toaster.

"Oh, I don't care, Nicky." Carolyn's voice slid like sweet honey through the telephone lines. "You have any suggestions?"

"Hmmm." Nick slathered a generous scoop of strawberry jam onto the bread's warm surface. "Well, Mike called. He and some of the guys are going inner tubing down the Stuck River. They asked if we wanted to go along."

"Ooh, sounds like fun," Carolyn squealed. "Let's."

"Okay. I'll fill the inner tubes and pick you up in about an hour." Nick responded. "Oh, and Carolyn," he added. "It might get a bit chilly when we're out on the water."

"Okay, I'll bring a sweatshirt."

Forty-five minutes later, crammed into Nick's little car alongside two puffy inner tubes, the young adventurers were on their way to Auburn.

Laughter and good-natured bantering greeted them as they pulled into the parking area alongside the Stuck River. Their companions for the day had already arrived and were eager to immerse themselves in the day's excitement. They quickly descended upon Nick's car, wrestling fat inner tubes from its interior and dragging them to the river's edge.

"This is going to be so fun," Carolyn whispered excitedly, tightening her fingers on Nick's arm.

One by one, members of the group launched their rubber vessels, slapping them into the water, flinging themselves into the slippery circles. While Nick positioned their own inner tubes along the river's edge, Carolyn slipped into an oversized, orange sweatshirt. Draping themselves across the inflated "doughnuts," they pushed away from the bank. As the swift current grabbed them, dragging them into the wake of the caravan ahead, Nick reached out and took hold of Carolyn's hand.

"Just so we don't get separated," he winked

For the next hour, the entourage turned and bobbed with a capricious current, at times drifting lazily through sluggish waters, at others, tossing wildly about, at the mercy of a turbulent river. They were nearing the bridge, their point of disembarkation, where transportation had been arranged to carry them back to their own car.

Nick tugged at Carolyn's hand, bringing their rafts close together. "You having a good time, Hon?"

"Oh, yes, Nicky." Carolyn's dark eyes sparkled. "Can we do this again? Soon?"

Nick's response was interrupted as the shouts and laughter of their fellow travelers, now ahead of them, drifted back from beyond a turn in the river. Rounding the bend, Nick and Carolyn discovered the cause for excitement. Stranded upon an isolated sandbar, tossed aside by the merciless river, shattered bodies of uprooted trees and broken limbs climbed upon one another, creating a water-soaked fortress. A frustrated current flailed and lunged at the logjam, seeking a way around the impassable barrier. Inner tubes became ammunition, missiles to be hurled, spinning and bumping against the logs before finally being released to more passive waters.

Now it was their turn. As the current snatched their craft, tugging, swirling them in opposite directions, Nick felt Carolyn's fingers slipping through his. "Hang on," he shouted, but the churning waters tore her hand from his.

"Nicky!" Shrieking with laughter, her eyes bright with excitement, Carolyn reached toward Nick's outstretched hand. Slapping the underside of the off-balance craft, an angry current roiled beneath them, dumping both tube and occupant into swirling waters, greedily sucking them beneath its surface. Though it seemed an eternity to Nick, in but a fraction of a second, the inner tube bobbed back to the surface.

Carolyn did not.

As if no longer interested in toying with its captives, the disgruntled current spewed the two inner tubes into quieter waters; first Nick's, then Carolyn's empty one. In the next instant, Nick was splashing across the sandbar's waist-high water toward where he had last seen Carolyn.

"Carolyn! Carolyn!" His frantic cries rose above the roar of the crashing waters. Panic sent adrenaline surging through his body as he clawed frantically at the pile of debris. Splintered branches slashed back at the bare skin of his arms and shoulders.

Frightened, their fellow rafters had scrambled to shore. Now they raced down the river's bank alongside Carolyn's drifting inner tube, hoping she, too, had been flung into quieter waters. But when they waded into the swirling eddies to reclaim her craft, there was no sign of Carolyn. Nick, teetering atop the slippery pile of debris, struggled in vain to dislodge the tangle of slimy logs. The agonized scream of a siren wailed in the distance.

Someone had called the fire department. Discarding their heavy gear as they scrambled from the fire truck, would-be rescuers recklessly flung themselves into the cold river, joining Nicholas in his frenzied efforts.

Someone had called the police department. Blue uniformed officers stood knee deep in the churning current, prying, tugging at an unrelenting captor. From somewhere, a chainsaw appeared to add its petulant whine to the unnerving cacophony of sound; the foul odor of its exhaust hanging heavy in the late afternoon air.

Someone called Nick's brother. Lee quickly joined his younger sibling upon the log jam but all efforts failed to produce any sign of Carolyn. Then, a fireman raised his arm, his shout halting the laboring rescuers. He'd caught sight of something orange. All eyes turned toward him, watching, waiting, hopeful. His arm dropped back to his side; he shook his head.

Carolyn's lifeless body had been found, the corner of her twisted, orange sweatshirt clutched in the relentless grip of a lifeless, splintered tree branch.

Chapter 24

In the bleak months following Carolyn's drowning, Nick struggled to focus again upon his life. But as fate robbed him of his true love, it also robbed him of his drive, his ambition. Drifting through a time of uncertainty and indecision, he met Mickey. Mickey was the complete opposite of Carolyn, in looks and personality. She was more gregarious, more outgoing, greeted life on a day to day basis with little concern for yesterday or tomorrow. Later, Nick would wonder if perhaps he sought solace in the arms of one so opposite, simply because she was so opposite, not only of Carolyn, but also himself. Whatever the attraction, he and Mickey were soon married.

With his zealous new wife at his side, Nick seemed to regain his old drive, his desire to excel. Together, he and Mickey embarked on a business enterprise utilizing Nick's talent and training in the field of art.

Before the end of the year, the business failed.

The marriage also failed.

* * * *

Once again, Nick found himself floundering in loneliness and indecision. It was Nick's brother, Lee, his strength at the riverside, who pulled him once again onto solid ground.

"There's a position opening up with the City Park and Recreational Department," his brother urged. "Why don't you put in your application?"

Nick was hesitant. "What kind of a job is it?"

"You'd be working with kids, developmentally disabled kids. I think you'd be good at it."

"Oh, I don't know, Lee. I've had no training in that sort of thing."

"Don't worry. They're not going to turn you loose without training. They hire primarily on the basis of personality and aptitude. I think you should give it a try."

It was with no small amount of skepticism young Nicholas filled out the pages of the application revealing the "who, why and wherefore" of his life to determine if he met the necessary requirements. His doubts proved ungrounded. He met the qualifications for the position. The job's responsibilities proved to be the perfect outlet for Nick. His old zeal resurfaced and he found himself able to connect with these "special" youngsters and they with him. His enthusiasm increased with his involvement in their sports program, in the supervision of their activities at summer camp. They became his family, his life.

* * * *

This morning was much like every other morning. In the few short years he'd been at this job, Nick found it seldom changed. The faces changed, some problems were more dramatic, but the perpetual never-ending effort to cope with the paperwork never varied. A frown dug at his forehead as he studied the weekly schedule of activities he had to fit into the inadequate budget. His scowl deepened as the phone rang, interrupting his train of thought.

"Hello!" he barked into the mouthpiece. "Nick here."

There was a pause at the other end of the line, then, "Hi, Nick."

His irritation gave way to a warm glow of pleasure at the sound of the familiar voice. "Sally!" It had been months since he'd heard from his once staunch friend and co-worker. Since job responsibilities sent each on their separate ways, they had drifted apart. "It's good to hear from you. How are you?"

"Oh, I'm fine, Nick. And you?"

"Just great. Couldn't be better."

"I heard about your promotion. Congratulations."

"Yeah, how about that? Who'd have thought they'd give me a raise just for playing games with a bunch of kids?"

"From what I remember, you're pretty good at it."

"Yeah, well…. Hey, Sal, I'm running late. Can I give you a call later … maybe we can get together?"

"Sure." There was a pause. "Nick, I'd like to talk to you about something."

Nick sensed a tension at the other end of the line. His voice shifted to the tone he used with his kids. "What's wrong, Sally?"

"I … It's … It's about my little girl."

"Gee, Sal, I didn't know you'd gotten married."

There was pause before the voice at the other end of the line responded. "I didn't, Nick. But Brenda, my little girl … she has a problem. There … there was an accident at birth." The voice grew tight with tears. "Nick, I know you work so well with … with the retarded …"

"Developmentally disabled, Sal." Nick's voice was stern. "Remember, my kids are only developmentally disabled. Look, I'll be back here about four. You remember where my office is?"

"Yes, Nick. I remember." It came as no more than a whisper, "Nick. Thank you."

✳   ✳   ✳   ✳

Nick looked down into the expressionless little face before him, the drooping eyelids, the slack-lipped mouth. Once again the surge of uncontrollable emotions raged through him; anger, despair, empathy. Another 'victim,' robbed by an accident of fate.

Pushing aside his feelings, Nick smiled. "Hi, Brenda. I'm Nick."

The blank little face stared back at him.

"I've shed so many tears, Nick. I don't want to put her in an institution, but...."

Nick slipped an arm about Sally's shoulders. "You've done the right thing, Sally. We'll take care of her. She'll be fine, I promise."

Taking her moist little hand in his, he gently turned Brenda away as her mother left the room. "You're mom will be back in a little bit," he soothed. "Meanwhile, there are some people I want you to meet."

* * * *

In the weeks and months that followed, Nick more than kept his promise. He took the little five-year-old under his wing, personally escorting her each day to the speech therapist, the reading classes, a personal hygienist. He took it upon himself to supervise her eating habits, aware that, as is typical in such cases, the appetite can be voracious, resulting in weight problems. Though Brenda continued to live with her mother, a bond was soon forged between Nick and his young ward.

Under the circumstances, it was only natural that Nick and Sally renew their old friendship. Job obligations still governed their relationship, but whenever possible, Nick and Sally spent time together, usually discussing Brenda and her progress. Then, when Brenda turned ten, Sally got married. This, in itself, did not disturb Nick; after all, theirs was merely a friendship. What did disturb Nick was the fact that Sally's new husband had definite reservations concerning Brenda and her place in their life.

"Look, Sal, how you run your marriage is your business but I refuse to stand by and let Brenda be put into an institution. She's come so far. She deserves a better deal."

Tears again spilled from Sally's eyes. "Oh, Nick, I don't know what to do. Steve can't handle the way Brenda is. But I love him." She met the anger in Nick's eyes then buried her face in her hands. "Oh, Nick, I love Brenda, too. But what else can I do?"

"You can appoint me as Brenda's guardian, that's what you can do." Nick countered. "Put me in charge of her care."

Nick turned the spare bedroom of his home into a child's room, filled it with stuffed animals, elementary level games and brightly colored accessories. Brenda often visited her mother and new stepfather, but it was Nick who made sure Brenda's holidays were spent with family, either Sally's or his own. He continued to work with the young girl, teaching her to swim, sharing his fishing expertise with her, even training her for the Special Olympics.

By the time she reached her twenties, though still limited in her capabilities, Brenda, could care for her own personal needs, print notes to her family. A two-day-a-week job at a Goodwill Store increased her feeling of self-worth. Best of all, she was able to move back with her mother once again. .

Nick continues to work with his "kids." His job has left him with little time to seek a lifetime companion. He is the last in the legacy of those sons called Nicholas who struggled through this family's history before him, each casting his own special shadow across the pages of America's evolution

978-0-595-45417-4
0-595-45417-8